Also by John Corry

Philosophy

The Wisdom of Love: Philosophical Implications of 1st Corinthians 13

Paul Among the First Philosophers: a symposium on Love

The Reconciliation of Paul and Nietzsche – a postmodern symposium on love and power

Primal Words: SELF, Love, God, Jesus

Bottoms' River

Christian Theology for Porn Lovers

Theological Reflections of a Catholic Quaker (essays)

Shimmering Words – a family of essays

Religion

Something to Offend Everyone – A Christian Life

Openings, Leadings, and Dreams: listening to the Inner Voice of Love

Forty-Nine Sits

John.... Yes Lord?

Talk with Jesus, and then Go Forward

[Should be another book like the last three talking-with-Jesus books]

A Short History of the Holy Spirit (2 volumes/ maybe be lost back in Tanguy)

God's Response to Satan's Holocaust: the clash between radiant goodness and radical evil

Prelude to God's Response to Satin's Holocaust

Radiant Church: Catholic, Quaker, and Bruderhof

Poetry

Heaven Our Last Beginning (a long poem)

Gospel Poems

Talimagala's Gift – Poems of Earth and Sky

Seeds of Sanctity

Travel

Three Cowboys Roam the Holy Land (with Jay Clark)

God and Art in Italy: bull sessions on the way to paradise (with Jay Clark)

The Spanish Connection (with Jay Clark, lost for now)

Plays

Save the Sardines

The Resurrection of Caroline Muse

Saints (one act play in *Emails, Letters and Limericks*)

Fifty Books

Author on Stage

Jesus on Stage

Bits and Pieces
Emails, Letters and Limericks
Still Writing at Eighty-Seven
Politics, Prayer, and Poetry

Metaphysical Mysteries
Bang!
Bang!Bang!

WHERE'S JESUS?

A METAPHYSICAL MYSTERY

JOHN CORRY

iUniverse

WHERE'S JESUS?
A METAPHYSICAL MYSTERY

iUniverse books may be ordered through booksellers or by contacting:

iUniverse
1663 Liberty Drive
Bloomington, IN 47403
www.iuniverse.com
844-349-9409

Because of the dynamic nature of the Internet, any web addresses or links contained in this book may have changed since publication and may no longer be valid. The views expressed in this work are solely those of the author and do not necessarily reflect the views of the publisher, and the publisher hereby disclaims any responsibility for them.

Any people depicted in stock imagery provided by Getty Images are models, and such images are being used for illustrative purposes only. Certain stock imagery © Getty Images.

Credits: front cover, Jesus Says Hi, saatch.com.
Back cover: author picture by Betty Jean Corry from Bang!

ISBN: 978-1-6632-5115-2 (sc)
ISBN: 978-1-6632-5116-9 (e)

Library of Congress Control Number: 2023903529

Print information available on the last page.

iUniverse rev. date: 04/27/2023

CONTENTS

"Sam"?

Nods.

"Remember the picture where one Image changes into another image"?

"Diptych"?

"A white tree in the center and if you look twice two women on either side".

"Except in our diptych if you look closely the two women are embraced by the figure of a first century Galilean healer".

"And some people see one image while others see two".

INTRODUCTION

<u>Old readers</u>

Welcome back to those familiar with the first two *Bang!* books who are ready, eager, can't wait, chomping at the bit to plunge back into the madcap metaphysical adventures of Swiss Madam President Hannah Hossenhoeffer and her four Stout Lads. Wigs the good-natured one, Hans the savvy one; Arnold Really O'Reilly unpublished mystery writer from windy northeast Maine, and professor Hank Hangover from Haverford college whose signature seminar *How to Love your Enemy in the 21ˢᵗ Century* is.

"Is what"?

"Just is".

"And other memorable characters. Including the evil opposition".

"Evil? Obnoxious, misguided, nasty, even criminal, but surely not evil. Evil titters on the edge of the fiery pit of eternal damnation".

"And a special welcome to newcomers who've come for the first time".

"How else would newcomers come but for the first time"?

Woof. Arf. Grrrr.

"That's Shatzi, a black and tan low bellied, short legged long dog – a dachshund - who interrupts when she's put off by la de da elitist wordplay or anything else that sparks her interest, tickles her fancy, scratches her funny bone, wets her whistle, takes the cake, or…"..

WOOF!

"What's the author like"?

"Tall, likeable, good looking, creative, dedicated…"

"No really".

"He's a bookish nerd with present urinary and past mental health issues. John has five children, one wife, and ten grandkids. He majored in philosophy, with a minor in English lit, which explains why he might write theological entertainments".

Pause.

"There are three levels to our story. The first on earth pits good guys just mentioned against bad guys and several nasty gals including… ".

Woof. Arf. Woof.

"The second level takes place on high in the one-time Home of the Gods, where Zeus and his entourage have been swept aside to make room for Sam an editor, Charly an author, and Caroline the Muse, who comment on the action below".

Pause.

"And the third level"?

"Is the offstage conflict between Radical Evil and Radiant Goodness".

FACT AND FANTASY

Fact

Berne, Switzerland, was founded in the late 12th century.

Tingle-Kringle is an indoor-outdoor café in Berne.

All food and drinks mentioned in the text have been consumed by real people.

All mountains and monasteries mentioned (except for Lucy Lucifer's *Silent Sisters Monastery)* have been climbed or lived in.

Swiss-German and other foreign words are, as far as the author knows, all used appropriately.

Swiss presidents serving one year at a time have far less power than Madam Presidents, Hannah Hossenhoeffer and Lucy Lucifer.

Fantasy

All notable characters and events are historically unverifiable.

To Be Determined

Does God exist?

PART I

CHAPTER 1

MAKE NEW FRIENDS BUT KEEP THE OLD

Bang!

"Stop!"

Bang!

"Stop damnit stop!"

"Too late Sam".

Bang!

"I quit. Be your own editor. You don't need me. I'm telling you Charly it's too much. It'll kill the first two".

"I changed the title Sam"?

"So what? It's still the third Bang! book. Same old characters. Same old plot".

Pause.

"How many times have you quit"?

"This time I mean it".

"Please Sam. Think it over. We've been together a long time. Remember the *Sardines*? They were good. Think it over".

Pause.

"Where's Caroline"?

"Here".

Caroline Muse not surprisingly is the Muse. She's been with Charlie and Sam since the first play; *Save the Sardines.* And the second The *Resurrection of Caroline Muse* when she was upgraded to the Higher Power before the Holocaust when she was demoted back to The Muse. It's unclear whether anyone's taken her place at the top spot since.

Pause.

[Lost bit of dialogue]

"Sorry. I can't help it, Sam".

"Whatta you mean you can't help it? You're the author. God, when there was a God, created the universe. Well maybe He did. Or She. Or It. Anyway authors create books without outside help. You think God created all the cheap junk people read? You're it Charly".

Pause.

"Can I tell you a story"?

"Can I stop you"?

"A young couple at a wedding reception hadn't been able to find a professional photographer so they provided miniature Kodak cameras for the guests to take pictures of the happy couple. Later when they went over the pictures there were pictures of the guests and their little party of family and friends. There were photos of dogs and flowers, well dressed children, the food table, the dancing, the smartly dressed servers, but none of the bride and groom.

"'Everyone sees the world from their own perspective.' Nietzsche.

Pause.

"Charly".

"What"?

"Don't blame Caroline".

"I do blame Caroline".

"Caroline proposes, I make suggestions, but you have the last word. And all the words in-between. I'm only Sam the editor. Caroline's the muse, but you're it Charly. Caroline, talk to him".

"I thought you quit Sam".

"Well I just un-quit".

***

Sitting alone outdoors at the *Tingel-Kringle* café in Berne, Switzerland, madam president, Hannah Hosenhoeffer, misses her old friends[1], the four Stout Lads. Wiggy Schlossenmeir-Bedfellow[2] the good natured one, and the saucy one Hans Yodelgruber Hassenfass have momentarily melted back into the characterless crowd. Arnold Really O'Reilly the would-be mystery writer is back on the windy coast of north-east Maine at his computer staring into space. Professor Hank Hangover is still teaching his signature seminar on *Loving Your Enemy in the Twenty First Century* at Haverford College in the… ".

Woof. Woof. Bowwowwow.

O and Schatzi an elderly black and tan Swiss dachshund who's an icon in dog world for her Berne to St. Petersburg overland run by night to save *Western Civilization* from Pastor Jones's unauthorized *Armageddon* is…".

***

"But now? Nada. Nothing. Damnit nothing!"

Hale and hearty Hannah sighed, pounded the table and ordered another Guinness and two birnhrot, the pear filled pastry she loved. One for now; one for later.

"I'm sorry madam we're out of birnhrot. Will fondu"?

---

[1] Most of the text is written in past time but occasionally, the author, slips ahead into present time.
[2] Schlossenmeir is Ludwig "Wiggy's", "Wigs", given name. Bedfellow is Wiggy's married name.

"Small portion".

"I'm sorry madam there is no small portion".

Pause.

Pause.

"Will there be anything else madam president"?

"Yes. Would you please ask Herr Glockenspeil to come out for a word. And Karl, don't leave. I have something to ask both of you".

Staring out across the stone street at the grim late medieval building across the way Hannah turned back to the waiter and his boss who was just returning with a polite but puzzled look. Alfons Glockenspeil, the owner, a short well-fed man wearing a charcoal and burgundy top of light gray lederhosen in his mid-fifties, had gray friendly eyes and a matching charcoal gray combover on top, was known for his ability to mix easily in all levels of society. And for his off-hours interest in the underside of European, especially Swiss, history.

"This table is too small, Herr Glockenspeil. Have you a larger one? For outdoors"?

"The conference table is inside madam but I'm afraid…".

"Please have it brought out".

When the large table, sitting eight, had been relocated to an airy environment Hannah asked her two guests to be seated.

"Please. Order Alfons's fondue of the day and white wine. I'll be back in a moment".

Then going table to table Hannah introduced herself to the few Swiss locals and a variety of foreign tourists and asked if they'd care to join her for Swiss fondue and a glass of white wine.

"I've ordered Blue Nun Rhine. It's cheap but the nun's my sister".

When two look alike six five coffee-colored lads in their early twenties and an older man from Tanzania, probably their dad, were joined by a family of four from Sioux City, Iowa, who reminded Hannah of a family she hadn't met, were seated Hannah stood and raised her glass.

"A toast to the future".

The Tanzanian trio stood at once and joined in the toast. The American family looked puzzled and remained seated; except for the little girl in blond pigtails about eight who stood, smiled, and drank the wine like Dr. Pepper, sputtered, choked and sat down as her mother pounded her back.

"Sorry".

Madam president sat, leaned in, and lowered her voice to avoid being overheard.

"My name is Hannah Hossenhoeffer. President of Switzerland. As you might expect…"

"Hans? What brings you here"?

Hans looked down at the little group and asked if he might join the party; then sat before anyone could respond.

Madam President continued.

"As you might expect I'm an organized person, an active person, a busy person; some say a bossy person. But today I'm not busy; I'm bored. Bored to the bone. That's why you are all here. To help me find my way out of…" Hannah shivered and suddenly realized *It's not just boredom Hannah. It's nothingness. Void.* Sartre's *Nausea.* T.S. Eliot's *Wastelands* and *more. The world is falling away*[3]*. And yet here are these strangers I've gathered looking to me for guidance,* and Hannah smiled and turned to the lighter option.

---

[3] Thoughts, poetry and quotes, appear in italics.

"Excuse me".

"Yes"?

The older man from Tanzania waited while a note quietly moved across the table to madam president who looked down then up, nodded approval and pointed to her right.

"The gent's in the back on the left".

When the older man returned the conversation had moved on to films and local entertainments madam might enjoy to lift her spirits, and soon after the party of eight said their goodbyes and went their separate ways. The American tourists to the *Paul Klee Museum* while the Tanzanian trio followed Hannah and Hans to the *Beastly Bottoms* several blocks away.

***

Hans, the smart one walking beside Hannah on their way to *Beastly Bottoms*, Berne's most controversial café, kept his voice low.

"Clumsy. Very clumsy. What were you thinking Hannah"?

"I lowered my voice but you're right. It was awkward. Do you think they noticed"?

"I'm sure they did. I recognized a woman from the embassy sitting at the table just behind you recording your low voice on a sophisticated cell phone".

Before continuing Berne's most bizarre bistro, *Beastly Bottoms* deserves mention. The idea had come up thirty years ago when the new owners of the bistro had little money left after essential expenditures to spend on the decorative ambiance every classy restaurant depends on to complement their cuisine. Browsing in one of the less expensive antique shops for mounted animal heads to fill the walls of their new bistro, and finding even these beyond their means, the new owners asked what happened to the rear ends of the sought-after Swiss mounted animal heads: the antlered red deer, shaggy brown bear, the Alpine ibex, and others. And so was born the eye-popping dining area of *Beasty Bottoms*. It was however after the re-greetings were over in the *Small Mammals* room in back, decorated with rodent rumps, beaver butts, and rabbit rears that Hannah's group settled down to discuss Hannah's quest for new life. While the others suggested various options Hale and Hearty Hannah took notes.

Take a trip. Go back to Cumru her hometown of four stone houses and a small church in Yorkshire, UK. In the States visit neo-Monet Longwood Gardens outside Philly, bursting with flowers and fireworks. Savanah Georgia, haunted by sea captains and suicides, windowless inner rooms, ghostly wisteria draped over cottonwood trees in the public plazas. And soft-spoken brown and black people who shared their won-hard faith to endure hard times in the dark forest with strange fruit hanging from white oak trees. Tanzania, Paris, Tibet. But no; it wasn't a change of scene Hannah was looking for. Inner peace perhaps?

An Indian ashram? A guesthouse on the sloping shores of Galilee. Thomas Merton's old monastery in Kentucky? Pendle Hill Quaker spiritual center outside Philly? A Native American Vison Quest? A Village binge in lower Manhattan?

CHAPTER 2

PLOT AND IDEAS

<u>Meanwhile</u>

Smiling to herself as she lingered over her coffee au lait, the young lady in the pink hat sitting behind Madam President's little gathering texted the embassy.

Code?

666.

Lucy?

H & H is bored.

How bored?

She's meeting with random strangers at the table in front of me. She wants their input on what she should do. The wire is getting most of it.

And?

And not much. Talk later.

Click.

Ninety minutes later.

"Any ideas"?

Back at the embassy Lucy Lucifer looked around the table.

"Ideas anyone"?

"Take her out".

Lucy who was chairing the little get-together shrugged a no.

"We have a cleaning lady on their staff. Zelma".

"And"?

"Sniff. Zelma Sniff".

Suddenly Lucy smiled that slow thoughtful smile that signaled the light was on. The doctor was in.

"What if someone new were to come into her life? A friend of a friend".

"What friend"?

Pause.

"Ludwig Schlossenmeir"?

"Wiggy?.... He is their weakest link. Good-natured. Gullible".

"And his weakest link is"?

"Zelda, his wandering wife, a willowy blond with a sleepy look and a slight lisp has been seen with Hans, Wiggy's best friend. And others".

"And Zelda's weakest link"?

"Tall, charming men modeled on Cary Grant".

***

"Zelda? Zelda Bedfellow"?

"Yes".

"Cary J. Alpine".

Brushing aside her long blond hair with a languid left-hand Zelda glanced up from the triangular hard glass table at the *Tringle-Kringle* outdoor café at the debonaire gentleman smiling down at her. She knew the name of course. Everyone in Berne knew C.J. Alpine, mountaineer and ace photographer. Six three, slim, with a pink scar across his sun-stained left cheek; black, gold stitched, lederhosen and suspendered white shirt, C. J. was known as Cary among his friends. There weren't many. Male or female. Admired for his glossies that appeared in all the best magazines and coffee table big books featuring snow draped peaks, deep rocky gorges, and an assortment of brown bears, alpine ibexes and European vipers, C.J. kept his cards close. Neither friendly nor unfriendly, most of C.J.'s life lay secluded behind his easy ways and a mildly sincere smile *kept himself to himself. Except. . . off putting e guthat like most mountain men Except for his long term laisons with. s brown bears, brownand breathtaking gourges, glossies in all the best magazines and coffee table big books like most mountaineers C.J. kept to himself except for the romantic liaisons with laisons e;t magazilnes y, C.J. like most mountaineers, suspended top bared half arms f armedsuspended red and white top.*

Woof!

"You've read my proposal"?

Zelda smiled. C.J. smiled. Like most celebrities Zelda and C.J. spend most of their public lives smiling.

"Yes. But no. I'm not interested in having my image momentarily lift the aging libidos of older men".

Zelda paused, looks down at her coffee au laud, then up, inhaling her *Ladies Light*, a trendy new brand from Norway promoted as "It's like breathing the Northern Lights".

"May I"?

When C.J. had seated himself just as Zelda was finishing her *Poire William*, a Swiss delicacy where pear seeds were allowed to ripen slowly inside a bottle...

"How else would fruit ripen but slowly"?

This from Sam, Charly's editor who with Charly – the author under another name -- and Caroline Muse, felt free to comment on the featured interactions in our fast-paced, riveting, non-stop, page turner narrative. Sam like Sancho Panza was a practical soul who kept his eye out - a painful simile – for misleading metaphors.

"Charly "?

"Yes Sam?"

"That's enough of that."

"I'll try."

Pause.

"Sam?"

"Ummm".

"Where does it end"?

"Where does what end"?

"Commentary on commentary. The labyrinth of language".

"Words float in limbo until they touch a particular reader's heart".

"Can we get back to Zelda and Cary"?

"They wander in space until…"

"You've said that already".

"This is a new thought; it needs elaboration".

Pause.

Pause.

"Sam"?

"Umm".

"Remember Plot and Wisdom? The two elements that drives any piece of narrative writing"?

"Or at least Ideas that might lead to Wisdom. So"?

"So, all plot and no wisdom and Jack's a dull boy. All wisdom and little plot and your book ends up in the Take One bin in second hand booksellers".

"Charly?"

"Yes"?

"So Plot and Ideas compliment but also compete for the reader's attention"?

"Yes, so we need to waste a few moments to let this new thought settle into the reader's consciousness. Take *'Parting is such sweet sorrow'*. Not of great interest to the gentle reader, until she's left standing alone at the airport waving goodbye to the departing jet. Or *'and I will luv you more my love till a' the seas gang dry'* that brings a teary smile when I think of Betty. Or *'Follow me'* that changed…"

***

Later that afternoon Zelda and Cary sipping *zuger kirschs*, a cherry flavored liqueur, at the *Paul Klee* museum café were easing their way toward a major obstacle to their budding romance.

"I'd never use your name and it's easy enough to alter your features. No one would ever know it's you"?

"I'd know".

Pause.

"Cary"?

"Yes"?

"I'll admit I find you attractive, but not enough to have my admittedly lovely body featured in an alpine setting".

"May I speak frankly"?

Zelda nods.

"I'm broke. I haven't sold a glossy in over six months. They say I'm not *au courant*. Everyone does the Alps, with mountain goats and mountaineers".

"And"?

Big sigh.

"And so I thought with an attractive…"

"A beautiful…"

"Woman to upgrade the Alps, I might get started again".

CHAPTER 3

FROSTY PHOTOS

"God it's cold. Hurry up".

"Almost done. Just one more".

Clickity-Click-Click-Click-Click.

"Ok, done. Wrap up. I have another surprise".

And so it was that Zelda and Cary, after a few shots on the lower slopes, were helicopterped up to the snowy peak of the *Jungfrau*. Theologically interesting the *Jungfrau* (*Jung* = young; *frau* = maiden = virgin = Virgin Mary) was named by nuns from *Interlaken Monastery* in the late 16th century. Later during the *Romantic* age Virgin Mary morphed into a high priestess; even a goddess. Paired with two neighboring mountains: *Monch* (monk) and Eiger (ogre), the three peaks side by side are physically awesome and metaphysically intriguing.

Meanwhile back on the Jungfrau Zelda and ace alpine photographer Cary were about to have their own physically awesome and metaphysically intriguing peak experience.

"Holy mothafucker. God it's cold. Hurry up Cary. I'm freezing".

"You're freezing. I'm frozen.....".

Pause.

Pause.

"Ah that's better. Thanks".

And so Zelda and Cary consummated their frenzied friendship while in the helicopter hovering above investigative reporter, Sky Wideeye smirked as he recorded the tender moment below on his Nikon Super-Zoom Digital camera.

***

"Sam what's your take on what we've just..."

"Forget it Charly. Stick with the Plot".

***

Two days later while Wiggy was out socializing with madam high and mighty Hannah Hossenhoffer, Zelda Bedfellow was upstairs in their apartment looking down on seven hundred years of Swiss history with the window closed. Bears! Smelly brown bears. There below were several uninformed archetypal Berne bears, symbol of a city whose image was imprinted on the city's, nay, the whole country's coat of arms; every letterhead, every postcard. Other countries had their eagles and lions or was it bulldogs but…

"Whoa John. It's just a couple of bears moseying about like bears will in any respectable zoo".

"Berne bears aren't like other bears. Ever since 1513, captured as the spoils of war, they celebrate the soul of a proud city, a proud canton, and ah yes, as capital of twenty six Swiss cantons, a proud nation. Without the bears the psyche of the nation is…"

Meanwhile.

"Not yet, John (author). You left Zelda back from the window sitting at her desk writing her anonymous memoirs, *The Misadventures of Madam Z*, while Hans was meeting with investigative helicopter co-pilot, Sky Wideeye, on a bench in *Kleine Schanze*, a small downtown public park. Sky, lean and fit in his late thirties had a Glint Eastwood look in his hard eyes that alerted Hans to the opportunity, or perhaps the threat, he sensed was coming.

Hans was one of the good guys, who sadly had a secret weakness for intrigue. It wasn't really the money. Well ok, money did enter into it; but Hans's overactive brain craved excitement and when the good guy adventures slowed down, Hans was drawn to a mini-mischief on the other side. So there he was sitting on a park bench listening to Sky Wideeye.

Without speaking Sky passed over the three glossy photos which Hans glanced at and returned.

"Why me"?

"I've heard you're savvy. I'd like your opinion".

"And perhaps my involvement"?

"Depends".

"As I see it I – we? – have two options".

"Which are"?

"A bidding war with the media. Or blackmail. I vote for the bidding war".

"There is a third option".

Sky waited, extracted an upscale blue English Rothman's from a slim silver cigarette case, inhaled in long even breaths, and looked out over the park.

Pause.

Finally Hans offered his own thought.

"You could secretly sign over the rights to *The Naked Jungfrau* to me, then make the best deal you can with the media moguls, before we renegotiate for a third more than the agreed upon amount".

***

"Charly "?

"Yes".

"What's a mogul"?

"Who knows. It's just a word that takes it's meaning from another word. Like Essequibo, a river in Quyana, or… need more help? – a small country on the northern Brazilian border. Many words depend on other words before they resonate with the ordinary citizen. Doctors, lawyers, and theologians each have their own private dictionaries which feed into humanity's large but limited linguistic library".

"Charly "?

"Without the words "female" and "male" endometrium (female) and Vas deferens (male) could refer to outlawing the metric system and the valiant defense of Schleswig-Holstein from the Danish hordes in 1848. In short any person, however knowledgeable, utilizes only a tiny fraction of the words available in humanity's linguistic library".

"So"?

"So how many body parts can you name? Twenty five? Fifty? How about seven and a half thousand? Not only are we physically mere specks in time and space, language-wise we are but microscopic leaves on the tree of knowledge.

"And mogul"?

"For those like me who need help, a mogul is a powerful autocratic figure like Genghis Khan the Mongol warrior or a bad-ass Hollywood producer".

***

Hans and Sky.

Hans. "Why would I give you rights to a million dollar plus expose"?

"Because I know the editor of *Blick* (*Peek, Glimpse*) would be interested in how you acquired the cash for your first helicopter".

Sky shrugs and his shoulders drop.

"You really are a sleazy bastard Hans. I don't know how Hannah puts up with you".

The wrangling went on for several minutes until Sky and Hans stood up and bumped knuckles. Sixty forty Sky, but Sky was already remembering the names of several of Berne's brighter private eyes. Aren't most? Private?

***

The Jungfrau (young virgin) rising slightly above its brother mountain, the monk, is of theological interest. Named by o untaiing slightly above it wGo aheadJungfrau. Named Jungfrau, young woman – virgin - by the nuns woman, o the virgin mountain by nuns at Interlaken Monastery from the nearby for a few glossy snaps of Zelda shivering in the thin sub artic air appeared in magazines and on T.V. all over the world.

***

Naked Jungfrau was selling well; Cary was away on a promotional tour in the States; Zelda was explaining to Wiggy that the revealing photos were produced in a purely professional manner when "O my God, the news broke. There on the front page of *Das Spiegel* was the to be celebrated photo of the snow topped Jungfrau, with a woman blissfully staring up from under the naked body of the mystery man, with the tattoo of a little legged low bellied long dog on his frosty left butt.

CHAPTER 4

ZELDA AND THE MYSTERY MAN

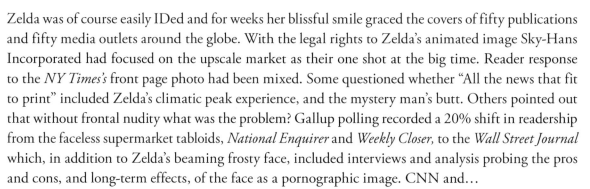

Zelda was of course easily IDed and for weeks her blissful smile graced the covers of fifty publications and fifty media outlets around the globe. With the legal rights to Zelda's animated image Sky-Hans Incorporated had focused on the upscale market as their one shot at the big time. Reader response to the *NY Times's* front page photo had been mixed. Some questioned whether "All the news that fit to print" included Zelda's climatic peak experience, and the mystery man's butt. Others pointed out that without frontal nudity what was the problem? Gallup polling recorded a 20% shift in readership from the faceless supermarket tabloids, *National Enquirer* and *Weekly Closer,* to the *Wall Street Journal* which, in addition to Zelda's beaming frosty face, included interviews and analysis probing the pros and cons, and long-term effects, of the face as a pornographic image. CNN and…

Woof.

"As I was about to say, CNN and the *Philadelphia Enquirer* hoping to stay ahead of the curve moved on to the mystery man with the tattoo of a black and tan little legged low bellied long dog on his left butt. And the word Jesus on his right. Which of course drew a mixed response from the religious community. Evangelicals were outraged or dismayed. Mainline pastors began their sermons by dismissing the tattoo as a distraction from preaching the Gospel. Whatever that might be. Some focused on verbal commitment to our Lord and Savior Jesus Christ; while others championed the works of mercy condensed to match the agenda of progressive Democrats, and still others far right and far left welcomed the tattoo, as either a miracle forced upon an ardent atheist, or C.J.'s secret commitment to the faith.

Philosophically inclined commentators discussed whether the bru-ha-ha over Zelda's and Bottom's Up frosty friendship reflects the unresolved dilemma of our generation. Did you not notice that even the most trusted names were suggesting that.…"

"No I didn't but I did notice that comedy, like science and poetry, is an intensely exact activity. One sneeze and microorganisms fly off the glass. One slip and boom; no more rocket, no more launching pad, no more…".

Woof

One misplaced word and the poem's dead. "In the room the women come and go talking of Cezanne? The fog creeps in on little dog's feet?'

WOOF!

"And comedy"?

"Same thing. Comedians in person and print craft their….

WOOF! ARF! WOOF!

"Sor-ry. I was just trying to broaden the conversation. Jeeze.

What's wrong with a little…"

***

Eventually of course *Bottom's Up* was traced back to C. J. but by then, since the critical photo legally belonged to Sky-Hans Inc., the big money was gone. Still, there were the bulky after-interview envelopes, and eventually Zelda and Cary sanctioned a documentary *Zelda and Cary on Top of Old Smokey* which was basically a repeat of the Jungfrau sensation. Other mountains…"

"Charly"?

"Fuji and the lower Himalayas"?

"You know…"

"I know. Quit while you're ahead. But I'm already a head".

Pause.

"Start over… Charly "?

"Yes Sam"?

"You've heard of the half-laugh? Humor is knowing when to quit. Now's the time".

***

Meanwhile Madam President, sitting with Wigs, was somewhere between furious and puzzled. What the hell was Hans thinking? Consorting with the *Dark Side*? Missing two *Beastly Bistro* back-room meetings? No response to emails? Or Facebook. Or Twitter. Or… when suddenly Hans appeared in the *Beastly Bistro's Small Mammals* backroom in a sharks' skin-colored Italian suit, collared with a beige and burgundy cravat.

"Where the hell have you been"?

"I was bored".

"So"?

"So I slipped over the border for a bit. I'm back home now, at your service".

Long pause. Waltzing in in a slick upscale Italian suit didn't sit well with Switzerland's First Lady. Hans had always been sly, but shark skins suits? Already a millionaire partnered with that snake in the sky, Sky Wideeye. Could he be trusted?

"Madam president. A word in private"?

Scrape, scuffle, flush. Waiting for a young lady with a large pink rose featured on her Libby Lib top to leave Madam President, turned over the sign on the Ladies door and waved Wiggy inside.

Hannah began.

"Yes"?

"Well, I was thinking. We have two options".

"Go on".

"If we don't trust Hans we can cut ties".

Up above the gods converse on the follies below.

"Charly"?

"Forget the ties".

"Or check out his sincerity and see what he's found out living on the dark side".

"How"?

"When he gives up his investment in Sky Snake's scam, and donates his Italian suits to Goodwill, he's back with us".

Neither of which happened. After conferring with Pope Philip it seemed that since any changes in Hans's finances or attire would be sure to be noticed it was better to maintain ties with Sky.

PART II

REFLECTIONS ON PART I

CHAPTER 5

CHARLY'S QUESTION

<u>Back upstairs</u>

"Sam"?

"Humm".

"Caroline"?

Nods.

"Where are we now? Plot and Idea wise"?

Sam: "Plot-wise the *Dark Side* is slowly evolving into a formidable threat to Hannah and her Stout Lads. Zelda's and C.J.'s reenactment of Shakespeare's *Beast with two backs* betrays poor Wiggy's trust. Sky guy's nose for nasty news leads to…"

Woof. Arf. Grrrr.

"Hans's holiday in hell with Sky leaves him…"

Grrr.

"And spiritually Lucy Lucifer's embassy of evil would weave all these random works of wickedness into a tawdry tapestry of temptation".

Pause.

"And Idea-wise"?

"Quite a few. Hannah's *Void* echoes T. S. Eliot's *Wasteland*; prelude to Enlightenment for some; conversion for others. It's the *Borderland* between the sensed universe and the unseen realm of uncertain certainty".

"The *Void* and"?

"Does God exist after the killing, the lies, the evil that poisons the air we breath? After Trump and Putin? After Satan's Holocaust"?

"Anything else? Besides Hannah's *Void*, and God".

"Why is Jesus tattooed on C.J.'s ass"?

"And the whimsical words on language"?

"Style. Nothing to do with content".

Long pause. Not because anyone missed the obvious connection between *Void* and God-Jesus but because they were pondering the effect of that obvious connection on the riveting storyline. Finally Caroline smiled.

"Que sera sera. N'est pas"?

***

"Sam"?

"What's on your mind"?

"What will be? What's next?

"Options. Options. So many options. What happened to the Tanzanian trio? How's Hangover's seminar on *Loving Your Enemy* going? Perhaps a murder or two? A marriage? A long interlude for The *Misadventures of Madam Z.* Accidents? Dissention in the Evil Embassy? Mental breakdowns?

"But the big one plot-wise is *Is Hans Yodelgruber Hassenfass on the level?* 70% - 30% so yes we'll stick with that and play out the conflict 'tween Sky Wideeye's greed and Hannah Hossenhoeffer's good guys".

"And Idea-wise"?

"Did the Holocaust delete God"?

CHAPTER 6

NEEDLES, THE KID, AND GOD'S RESPONSE TO SATAN'S HOLOCAUST

"No. I'm sorry Cary; but no".

***

Without looking up Needles, an old man with a faded purple patterned oriental scarf around his thin veined neck and a dusty black beret on top, put down the bottle and snarled.

"We're closed. Go away".

"I have money".

"I don't give a shit whatchagot. You're too young. I'll lose my license".

Standing in front of the still quivering beaded curtain was a kid Needles had never seen before. *Twelve, maybe thirteen, with a couple a crumpled bills clutched in his right hand. Good looking kid. Had too much to drink. Shit I've had too much to drink. We'll get along fine.*

Long pause. The beaded curtain came to a stillness.

"Comeonin. Take a seat".

The kid sits and looks around. Stained with smoke from years of scorched flesh the walls divided unevenly into three parts. One wall was covered with esoteric symbols; knives, dragons, snakes, crafty crouching Gollum, and so on. On the second symbols and scenes were religious. Some of Buddha, lotus flowers and the sangha (Buddha's little gatherings of fellow seekers for Enlightenment). Other tattoos pictured the Virgin Mary, the heavy cross and the lighter cross. A few pictured Christian scenes. Paul falling off his horse. St. Francis talking with Jesus on the cross in the shabby chapel in Damien. The third wall was festooned with roses, flowery wreaths, and "Mother", "Betsy", "Babe", and "Dude".

"How much ya got"?

"Enough". And he put the money back in his jeans.

Smart kid. Needles was curious.

"Whadayawant? Snakes? Crossed daggers? A boney white skull with witch haunted eyes? Grim grinning *Gollum*"?

"Somein' different. Unique. Someplace my parents won't find it".

Reaching back into a pile of old books Needles fumbled for a puffy covered shabby copy of *Roses, Hearts, and Snakes: The Big Book of Tattoos*.

"Kid, you're underage. I could lose my license".

"You said that already".

Sassy kid. I like him.

"Come back in a couple of years".

And so it transpired that young Cary bared his bottom and Needles burned a low-bellied, little legged sausage dog on Cary's left butt and, God knows why, the word *Jesus* on his right butt.

***

On his eighteenth birthday Cary's butt puzzled the Army's induction doctor, who orders a psychological examination to determine how young Cary might best serve the needs of the nation. When the test results and interviews with Cary, family, and friends prove inconclusive Cary's future is left in the hands of three experts: Doctor Noitall, professor of philosophy and religion at the University of Zurich, David Hart a Jungian analyst from Lucerne, and Frau Poochie director of the nation's top dog pound in Berne. Frau Poochie, who doesn't like slackers, suggests young Cary would make a great pooper scooper and general handyman at the dog pound in the low rent district of Geneva. David Hart recommends Cary spend his eighteen months serving his country as a dishwasher at a homeless shelter in Zurich, and Dr. Noitall would have Cary serve as an assistant grave digger in *Silent Sisters*, a break-away independent Carthusian Monastery not far from Lucerne. Trusting his intuition that the right buttocks was the right buttocks, Cary opted for the monastery.

***

"So"?

"Too early to tell".

Seated with her friends around a wobbly wooden table that had replaced the…

Woof.

Madam President grinds her teeth, sighs impatiently, and stirs her cup of cold cappuccino. Hans looks up at the tail feathers of the latest addition to the *Small Mammals Room*; a *Bearded Vulture*, a large predator who lives largely (80% to 90%) on the bones of small mammals. Wigs[4] sips his lukewarm Swiss Coke. Madam President stops stirring. Wiggy puts down his Coke. The room settles into stillness. A lone fly circles the restricted space looking for a…

"Flies don't look".

"Searching"?

"Flies do look. In all directions. Mostly colors".

---

[4] Ludwig Schlossenmeir Bedfellows is the good-natured one. His buddy Hans Hassenfass is the smart but saucy one.

The buzzing silence continued until the ring-tone of the Swiss national anthem signaled…
"When the morning stars grow red, and o'er us their splendor spread, Thou O…"

**

Meanwhile looking down on Hannah and her two stout lads Sam and Charly ponder the relationship between the Lucy Lucifer's Evil Embassy, the reference to Jesus which led C.J. to Satan's immoral monastery and…
"Has God survived the Holocaust"?
Sam and Charly turn to Caroline, the Muse, who nods and the discussion begins.
"Caroline"?
"Yes Sam"?
"About the Holocaust"?
Pause.
The fly lands on Sam's nose.
"Shoo". Sam brushes the fly away. The fly circles the room and again settles on Sam's nose.
Pause.
"Charly you remember. We saw the rerun".[5]

**

---

[5] Chapters three through five, eighty-seven pages, in the author's *God's Response to Satan's Holocaust; the clash between radical evil and radiant goodness* present evidence that God *did* respond to Satan's Holocaust.

Oscar Schindler and Ann Frank's are only two of the millions who responded to the Holocaust in caring and courageous ways. Dutch bishops, the Danish king, the Belgium queen and a majority of the population of Denmark, Albania, Finland, Belgium, Holland, and surprisingly Mussolini's Italy supported or actively protected Jews against the "German disease".

"When five thousand villagers from Le Chambon-sur-Lugnon and several neighboring villages were asked to shelter hunted Jews by their pastors Andre Trocme and Edouard Theis they responded by caring for some 3,500 Jews over a period of several years". [Martin Gilbert, *The Righteous – the Unsung Heroes of the Holocaust*, Henry Holt & Co., 2003]

"On February 27th, 1943 the Berlin Gestapo rounded up 4,700 Jewish men married to Aryan wives. When they were placed in a detention center on the Rosenstrasse waiting to be sent to their death several thousand gentile wives appeared in front of the building demanding their spouses release. By nightfall they were joined by several thousands more who stood with them for a week in the cold winter weather until the men were released by Goebbles as 'privileged persons… to be incorporated into the national community.'" [*The Righteous*, Page 191-2]

"At all levels of society Belgium responded as a culture of hospitality, which saved half of the Belgium Jews. In September 1943 when six Jewish leaders were arrested Queen Mother Elizabeth, and Cardinal van Roey, head of the Catholic church in Belgium intervened to obtain the release of five of the Jewish leaders… *Queen Elizabeth Castle*, a home for children of Belgium soldiers, sailors, and airman, took responsibility for sheltering eighty renamed Jewish children until the end of the war. Cardinal Roey was also active protecting Jews in orphanages, geriatric centers, and other institutions under his control. In Belgium as in Holland, Albania, Finland, and Denmark it was,

"Sam…. What's the difference between religious folks and humanists"?

Pause.

"Religious folks believe a lot of stuff that's up for debate".

"Seriously".

"Humanists believe in what you can see, touch, and measure. 'No truth but in things.'"

"And religious folks believe in what you can't see, touch, or measure? Two realms of reality. Earth and God's other world. Heaven. Right"?

"Right".

"What's Heaven like"?

"Better than here".

"So if someone dies they go to a better place"?

"I guess".

---

with sad exceptions, the entire population of a nation that risked their lives to defend the Jews". [*The Righteous*, Pages 318-319]

"The German ambassador in Bulgria responding to what was known as the '*Miracle of the Jewish people*' in the capital *Sophia*, Bulgaria's successful objection to Hitler's racial policies, which would have sent 48,000 Jews to their deaths, wrote that the Bulgarian population 'lacked the ideological enlightenment we have… and does not see in the Jews any flaws justifying taking special measures against them". [*The Righteous*, p. 249]

"In Hungary the military, including dictatorial Admiral Horthy who reigned as Regent for several decades, the Red Cross, certain Protestant and Catholic leaders, and Swedish diplomat Raoul Wallenberg who organized a network of 400 rescuers who rescued a quarter of a million Jews from deportation, all did their best to rescue Jews. In Budapest Wallenberg saved 69,000 Jews housed in the Big Ghetto by threatening to expose the German general who was about to order their massacre as a war criminal. Another 25,000 Jews were secluded in churches and private homes. In Budapest itself 50,000 Jews were saved. Sadly outside the capital two thirds of Hungary's 750,000 Jews were sent to the death camps or murdered by local antisemites, the vicious Arrow Cross". [*The Righteous*, page 249]

Other references that support the thesis that a Higher Power responded to Hitler's Holocaust include Irene Gut Opdyke's *In My Hands – Memories of a Holocaust Rescuer*, 1999; Eva Fogelman's *Conscience and Courage*, 1994; Radolf Braham's *The Politics of Genocide*; Martin Buber's *Witness to the Holocaust*; Rochelle G. Saidel's *The Jewish Women of Ravenbruck Concentration Camp*, 2001; *Different Voices: Women of the Holocaust* 1993; Yaffa Eliach, Hass, *Hasidic Tales of the Holocaust*, 1982; and Pesach Shindler's *Hasidic Responses to the Holocaust in the Light of Hasidic Thought*, 1990.

"For the first fifty years after the Holocaust survivors bore witness to evil, brutality and bestiality. Now is the time for us in our generation to bear witness to goodness, for each of us is living proof that even in hell, even in that hell called the Holocaust, there was goodness, there was kindness, and there was love and compassion".

Abe Foxman, Holocaust survivor and national director of the Anti-Defamation League for eighteen years

"Life in Ravensbruck took place at two separate levels, mutually impossible. One the observable, external grew every day more horrible. The other, life we lived with God, grew daily better, truth upon truth, glory upon glory".

Corrie ten Boom - Christian survivor

"Even Hitler? What happens to Hitler and the other monsters? Attila, Jack the Ripper, the Kansas City bomber? What happens to them"?

Woof. Arf. Woof.

Caroline lowered her head and withdrew into silence. Sam waited. Charly waited; until finally Caroline put her arm around Sam and took Charly's right hand.

"I'm sorry Sam; I can't tell you".

"But there is an answer"?

"O yes there's an answer".

"Then why not tell us"?

"Because it would distract you from your own journey… Charly "?

"Yes"?

"Do you need an answer"?

"Well I'm curious of course, but no I don't need an answer".

***

Will there be cold beer in heaven for Americans? And tea for the rest of the world?

How many gnats does it take to dance on the point of a pin before one is bumped off?

Do dreams ever really come true? And would you opt in if they did?

And now for something completely different.

Woof. Arf. Woof.

"Yes"?

"…….. ….. …………… ……! …………. ….. ……".

"Slow down…"

"Yes….. Yes…. You're sure?... No… No… Not yet…. Good work. Thanks".

Bang! Hands slam down on the hard oak table. Madam President beams and rings for the waiter.

"Bitte!"

"Yes Madam President"?

"Champagne. Your best for the boys. Under forty euros. And Guinness for me".

Pause.

Hans. "So"?

"So my cheeky friend C.J. has made contact with our agent in the Silent Sisters Monastery who tells him Needles tattooed *Jesus* on the young guy's butt without his permission".

"And"?

"And no one knows why. My guess is he could see the kid would need help. Brash, good looking, the kid would definitely stand out".

"So the tattoo is his protection"?

"Could be".

"What else didya learn"?

"Over half the monks and staff at Silent Sisters Monastery have ties to the Evil Embassy. Lucy Lucifer visits her son the abbot Bells Z every week".

"Why a monastery?

"No one's allowed to visit a Carthusian monastery. *Strict Rule*: no visitors, restricted diet: barley biscuits and prunes; abbot's word is law; light whipping for penance, silence except for hymns at Mass. Perfect cover for Lucy L. to plan her next move".

***

Swishwack! Swishwack! Swishwack!

"Speak you miserable toad".

Swishwack! Swishwack!

Lucy put down the knotted whip and walked around in front to face C.J.

"Talk or I'll beat the living shit out of you? What's Hannah planning? Is the pope involved"?

Silence.

CHAPTER 7

BACK TO THE PRESENT

T'was a balmy day in May when Madam President Hossenhoeffer held court outdoors at the Tringle-Kringle café. As the assembled notables: Hans Yodelgruber, Wiggy Schlossenmeir-Bedfellow, professor Hank Hangover on sabbatical from *The States*, and Arnold the unpublished mystery writer from the chilly March rocky coast of northeast Maine were settling into their afternoon schnapps and petit-fours, Hannah looked over her notes.

Problem: Sky-Hans' monopoly on the rights to the notorious *Naked Jungfrau* photos was raising billions, two thirds of which, unknown to Hans, Sky had siphoned off to an independently operated Carthusian monastery associated with the *Evil Embassy*.

Solutions:

Wiggy. Madam President Hannah unofficially negotiates for a fifty-fifty split with Sky-Hans Inc. Hans uses his influence to persuade Sky to go along. [No reason for Sky to voluntarily give half his earnings to anyone. Shows weakness.]

Hangover-O'Reilly joint suggestion: Threaten Sky-Hans with legal action based on vague statutes against using Swiss air space as one's personal property. "Swiss air not for Sky". [Could lose. Long trial exposes the government to attacks from media and political adversaries. Progressive agenda abandoned].

Hans. Kidnap Sky implicating Putin? Taliban? C.I.A? Al-Qaeda? Mossad? [no evidence. Risky public relations-wise.]

My imput. 1. More schnapps; more discussion.

2. Nap and reconvene for a night out on the town.

And so it was agreed they'd meet at Berne's newest night spot, "The Zoo for You". No cell phones, no political conversation, no mention of the Jungfrau, helicopters or Zelda.

***

Jumpin' jellybeans what a night. It started with Madam President's party of five slipping quietly through the rose flowered arch into a free range mini-zoo where Berne's work-worn weary elite relax in the company of several foot high Little Blue "Fairy" penguins, two young koala bears, a family of black and tan low-bellied little legged dachshunds, and various dogs, cats, and hamsters owned and cared for by the owner and staff of *Zoo for You*. Over drinks; Guinness for...

Woof.

"Why Woof? I was interested in the conversation"?

Woof........ sorry...... Woof.

Guinness for Hannah. Hans and Wigs coax Arnold and Hank Hangover to try the popular Swiss fruit brandy Apriocotine and the next two hours were spent patting pets, sipping sweetness, and conversing in low tones on the differences and similarities between Swiss, American and Yorkshire weather, geography, politics, taste in food, music, and dating patterns. Shortly after 11: 00 Hannah and Arnold left while Hans, Wigs, and Hank went on until 2: 00. Ah youth when lads and lassies of yesteryear whiled away the waning hours till dawn broke out like thunder China cross the bay.

CHAPTER 8

THE GREAT DEBATE

Meanwhile Lucy and the *Evil Embassy* had not been idle in their quest for chaos. After the obvious options had been eliminated: encourage Putin to employ surgical nuclear attacks on EU centers of power: Brussels, Berlin, Paris, and Rome; circulate rumors of space aliens masquerading as diplomats, doctors, and Democrats; and for hard right Evangelicals to assassinate the pedophile pope to initiate Armageddon. Lucy called for other options.

After ten minutes of intense discussion it was agreed that Lucy herself was the obvious choice to lead the charge by running for president in the next election. Deleting Lucy's surname (Lucifer) in favor of Koenig (king) Lucy Koenig was ready to go.

***

Time passes uneventfully until it's time for Madam Hossenhoeffer to run again as president of Switzerland's twenty-six cantons. "Thank you Gretchen. In my closing remarks as your past president I'd like to stress that I'm the only one on this stage who has the experience and wisdom to guide our beloved homeland through the trying year ahead. Let us look at the clear choices that separate Ms. Koenig and myself. Lucy has aligned herself with Gadamer Putin. She threatens to take Switzerland out of the EU. Lucy's tax plan I must admit *would* lower your taxes to almost nothing. Nothing for nothing. No public education; no day care centers, no military to defend the homeland. Public libraries closed; police replaced by private security services paid for by individual citizens, no government regulations to protect the public from contaminated meats and vegetables. The choice between myself and Ms. Koenig is clear. Continuation open to reasonable responses to new challenges. Or chaos. I look forward to your support at the polls. Thank you very much".

"Thank *you* Madam President".

Pause.

"Ms. Koenig".

"Thank you Gretchen. Your evenhanded support for my opponent has been obvious throughout this farce of a debate. The lines however had been drawn well before my opponent and I ever walked onto this stage. Polls show homebodies over fifty will support my illustrious adversary by a wide margin. Polls also show her support is waning among younger voters with the largest number of undecideds in recent history. This election is about two individuals. Who do you trust? Who do you feel has a better sense of the future. Let us look at my illustrious opponent's record. Born in the UK, she speaks movingly of 'Switzerland, my homeland'. Forgoing good Swiss snapps she drinks only Irish beer. Making only token appearances with the cabinet and other state officials she relaxes and makes policy in the backroom of the notorious *Beastly Bottoms* with the unelected, unappointed *Gang of Four*. A clueless unpublished *American* mystery writer. A whimsical *American* professor who preaches pacificism. Two Swiss twofaced opportunists. Hans Yodelgruber a loyal supporter of the president and millionaire co-owner in Sky Wideeye's pornographic enterprise. And Wiggy Schlossenmeir-Bedfellow who pimps for his high-flying floosy wife Zelda. The choice is clear. Vote for a past cradled in corruption or vote for change. Vote for a sunlit dawn to brighten our dark past. Vote for Lucy Koenig the only real Swiss candidate. And let the party begin.

***

Though the winner was not announced until the wee hours of...

Woof.

...unfortunately for our heroes the party-loving "What the hell. It's only for a year" vote flipped the switch to Lucy, and a new era in Swiss life began. Wow, what a...

Ahem. Woof.

"But..."

"Briefly. What a... one word"?

"Disaster".

The money previously spent on public services was used to promote public spectacles long remembered as *Medieval Madness*. At first the feudal folk dress and dancing, jousting, and log tossing contests held the public's attention but when Madam President introduced schnapps induced vomiting competitions and a bloody reenactment of the William Tell saga her ratings dropped in the polls. And when her twin sister, if it was her twin sister, was photographed at three AM on a moon-lit night inspecting the *New Berne Waste-Water Treatment* plant prior to an outbreak of dysentery, hepatitis, and Typhoid fever the public had had enough. Shortly after dark a raucous torch bearing Frankenstinian vigil was held outside the president's residence, and during the day a parliamentary panel was convened to begin impeachment proceedings against Madam President "on suspicion of serious breach of duty". On the opening day however Madam President failed to appear and her mysterious embassy had a **For Sale** sign on the spacious front lawn. Rumors unconfirmed to this day suggest that...

Arf... move on... Arf

***

Like Greek gods suspended above the worldly woes below Sam, Charly, and Caroline discuss which woe most merits immediate attention.

Sam. "After Lucy's *Medieval Madness* and overtime for hospital healers coping with water poisonings Switzerland is broke. Our first concern must be for reinstated Madam President Hossenhoeffer to revive the economy".

Charly. "In real time yes, but this is a story, Sam. Fiction. Fantasy. Somewhere between the sharp-edged reality of our waking hours and the fleeting dreams of restless sleep. Reader interest will surely focus on the flashback to the immoral monastery where Lucy is still swishwacking the tattooed word "Jesus" on poor C.J.'s rosy-red butt".

Pause.

"Caroline? What's your view"?

"I'd begin with Hannah's secret agent in Lucy's evil empire to see if she might save poor C.J. from Lucy's vicious beating".

***

Back in the devil's monastery's supply room Lucy's voice over the intercom cackled with delight. "Send down the death whip. The spiked one with notches on the handle".

"I'll go" the latest recruit sighed and holding the leathery lash lightly the tall, blond hooded figure limped down the stone stairs to the dungeon below where Lady Lucy, sweaty and naked from the waist up, was hovering over a man tied face down on a narrow black leather bench. Without turning around Lucy reached for the lash behind her, but instead of the deadly last lash Zelda grabbed Lucy's hand and jerked her across the room where she lay crumpled on the floor as Zelda covered her face with a chloroform rag. Then wrapping C.J. in her dark cloak the two alpine celebrities escaped through secret passageways back to the free world.

***

Hale and hearty Hannah wriggled her shoulders and settled into the comfy ash gray swivel presidential chair. *A new day ahead. Let us wake with a winged heart and give thanks for another day of loving. Gilbran.* She sighed and looked out the wall-wide window over her beloved Berne. *The old town clock still keeping time as the city grew and grew from its late medieval beginnings, the two rivers circling the Old City with...*

"Madam president"?

"Yes Greta"?

"Only three today".

"Yes"?

"Developers in Speitz[6] have acquired land by the lake to put up an amusement park".

"Have the Secretary of the Interior investigate and present me with doable options. No more than three".

Pause.

"The Paul Klee museum is planning to sell Klee's *Head of a Man* to the Met".

"One of his best... When do they sign"?

"Next Thursday".

"Call Gustav and set up a meeting tomorrow. At his convenience in my office".

Pause.

---

[6] *Speitz on Lake Thun* is one of Switzerland's most historic and scenic sites.

Hannah sighs and turns the comfy swivel chair to look out the window again. Spread wide around her were eight centuries of the old Zytglogge (Clock Tower), Saint Peter and Paul's cathedral, and all the homes, shops and public buildings nestled in the old city shaped like a stubby penis nestling serenely in the Aare river. *Such an old city. No, not just old. Ancient. Hallowed by the lives of industrious citizens who built and maintained the necessities of civilized life for centuries. Hallowed by neighborly interactions: neighborly get-togethers, festivals, sports events, common worship, music, and art. And then the other events mellowed by memory: harsh words and angry fists in the family, religious contention, political and financial corruption undermining our image of the peaceful city set among the mountains while the world wars below.* And Hannah thought of the Swiss banks that funneled Jewish fortunes into the hands of the Third Reich, and still serve as conduits for powerful parties who wish to keep their financial affairs unpublicized. And yet what city is not stained with events which do not appear in their promotional brochures? Each city on earth is a microcosm…

Woof.

A microcosm of…

ARF!

Madam President yawned, turned away from the window, and lifted the anatomically accurate Berne bear beer mug in Greta's direction.

"I shoulda hired you years ago, Greta. What's the third item"?

"Someone named Needles has something he wants to share. It's about Cary Alpine's butt. Privately".

Hannah and Greta smiled across the Swiss president's slick mahogany desk.

Pause.

"How'd he contact us"?

"By phone".

"How'd he sound"?

"He sounded excited in a positive way".

"Age? Educated"?

"Seventies? Yes, but he smokes too much".

"Check him out and if he's for real tell him to hail City Cab 719 outside the main library next Tuesday at 11:00".

"And then"?

"I'll worry about that. O and I'll have another cappuccino".

***

"Mr. Needles"?

"Just Needles".

Pause.

Looking around the Small Mammals room at *Beastly Bottoms* Needles, was so absorbed in picturing how the bottom half of the small mammals that lined the walls might enrich his tattoo business, he'd momentarily forgotten why he'd come.

"Needles".

"Yes mam".

"You've come quite a distance to tell me something. What is it"?

"I wonder if I might have something to drink first. Just to steady me nerves". When Needles' nerves had settled Madam President repeated her question.

"Correct me if I'm wrong but as I understand it, when a twelve year old who's not used to strong drink comes for a tattoo, you stitch a dog on his left butt and the word Jesus on the other half. Where'd that come from"?

Needles grinned and pulled out a tattered oversized book on tattoos. Opening the book to a page near the back he handed the book over to Madam President and put his right index finger on the passage in question. Then sitting back he resumed inhaling on a short stubby cigarette.

"The astute tattoo artist after mastering the standard symbols of his craft will be open to those unrecorded images that appear in dreams".

Hannah looked up. "And your dream was"?

"I'm at the Westminster dog show when the dogs break their leashes and turn on their trainers snarling and biting. Then the scene changes and a spotted black and tan dachshund eludes the hunters who are chasing her by hiding in a secluded cave which morphs into St. Francis's chapel in the woods outside Assisi. When the dog fades I'm standing in the back of the chapel facing Jesus himself, who's replaced the wooden crucifix of Christ on the Cross. Then the dream fades".

Long pause.

"So you thought…"

"When this smart-ass kid comes in why not tattoo the dog on one side and Jesus on the other".

CHAPTER 9

FOLLOW THAT DOG

It was a dark and cloudy afternoon – 5 below outside - in the Really O'Reilly's Cape Cod cottage as the Swiss visitors: Hannah, Hans and Wigs, and three Norbertine newcomers: Sister Phyllis, Brother Andrew, and abbot Joel[7] from the abbey outside Philly, and Josephat (Hossie) Corrie were toasting nicely by a roaring fire in front and four surrounding space heaters behind, while Hannah prepared to present her proposal. Until Hans asked about the American Norbertines.

Sam to Charly. "Footnote"? [8]

Pause.

"How long"?

"Moby promised heat by early afternoon tomorrow".

Pause.

Sensing the question before it was asked host Arnold Really O'Reilly explained.

"Power outages are common into April. We keep sleeping bags handy in case we have sleepovers but you all are used to wintery springs. Shouldn't be a problem. Now can we get to work"?

***

"Sam"?

"Ummm".

"I'm wondering if we aren't overdoing the list of names thing".

"But won't it…"

"We clog up every scene change with who's there. Why not let the characters just talk".

---

[7] Abbot Joel is wise, good-natured and about 6 foot 3 with a pink scar across his left cheek from an old college fencing mishap.

[8] "Sister Phyllis, the first female Norbertine in eight hundred years, is a middle-aged housewife whose husband served as the American doctor keeping an eye on Pope John Paul II".

"And what did *Phyllis* do?"

"Sister Phyllis is a three term president of the *PIW, Priests-in-Waiting.*

"And trust readers will catch on"?

"Worth a shot".

***

With no objections Hannah stated the challenge.

"Now we've solved the mystery of C.J.'s bottom ".

"Which is"?

"Since the dog on one side leads to Jesus on the other why not follow the dog to find Jesus"?

Pause.

Pause.

"Which dog? There are tons of dogs to choose from"?

Pause.

"Why the switch"?

"What switch"?

"Critiquing the metaphors. *Worth a shot? Tons of dogs?* You let it pass".

"I couldn't keep up. We're immersed in metaphors. We couldn't communicate without them".

"Metaphors are polluting the language with misinformation. Dogs aren't counted by tons".

"But everybody understands. It's the way we communicate".

"Our generation maybe, but the next generation invents their own metaphors and…"

"Is that such a bad thing? Allows room for each wave of new citizens to modify the language. Make new words but keep the old".

"It's not the words; it's the phrases that matter. We speak in phrases".

"Sentences"?

"No phrases. We write in sentences; we speak in phrases".

"Can we get on with it"?

Pause.

"Before we get *back on track* may I make a suggestion"?

Pause.

"Why not provide footnotes for those who need them"?

"You mean those who can't keep up"?

Wisely, leaving that last comment unanswered, the group moved on to the plot-relevant portion of our riveting narrative. After ten minutes of concentrated conversation it was agreed that Schatzi, the little legged, low-bellied canine heroine of European dog lore for saving Western Civilization from Pastor Jones's Armageddon in *Bang!* would sniff out the elusive Jesus from among the eleven plus billion human souls on earth.

Short pause.

"Schatzi will need help".

"Which means a list…"

"A fairly extensive list of Schatzi's helpers. Each with a certain area of expertise".

***

"I thought we ruled out long lists".

"Can't be helped, Sam. What do you think Caroline"?

Pause.

"Remember the lumberjacks"?

"No".

"Guiding the logs downstream? Jumping from one log to another. Poking the logs apart with a spiked pole to prevent jams?... Sometimes we have to change plans to keep things moving".

***

Two weeks passed until FJC, the *Finding Jesus Committee,* convened in one of the smaller Vatican conference rooms with Pope Phillip Neri in attendance.

"Who is"?

"Bob Williams, a lifelong Lobos fan from Albuquerque who visits his spiritual director, Michelangelo's ceiling in the Sistine Chapel, every week or two depending on…

Woof. Arf. Woof.

"Pope Philip's best friend and advisor is abbot Joel whom we've already met".

"But not for a while".

"Joel's a Norbertine…"

"A what"?

"Saint Norbert, a precursor to Assisi's saint, was another wandering evangelist who favored the poor".

"Precursor? What's a …"

"And Joel"?

"The pope's friend from before the seminary. They have a long history together beginning with…"

Woof.

"The pope dating Joel's sister he'd met in Taos on a ski week…"

ARF!

"Who's Philip Neri"?

"Philip Neri is the trickster patron saint of Rome. He kept his more self-centered followers in line by having them carry a pig under their arm in public. He himself often wore only a half a beard and kept a book of jokes with him to lighten the tone of his work among the poor and the pilgrims who flooded Rome at that time. A charming saint who hid his good works under a cloak of clownishness. Philip Neri reminds me of St. Francis who appeared naked in public and referred to himself as "donkey dung".

Pope Philip, sobered by his papal responsibilities unlike his namesake, has modified his earlier clownish ways. He listens well and consults seriously with his advisors, but unsullied silliness still surfaces from time to time. Following conservative pope *John Paul III,* who modeled himself on his personable predecessor *J.P.II,* pope *Philip* represents a return to the Vatican II agenda of engaging in dialogue with the world. Occasionally his basic trust in that of God in every human being leads the pope to overlook the evil that lurks in hearts of men, and occasionally women as well. All in all, Pope Philip Neri is what progressive Catholics call a "Good Pope".

The conference room itself, recently renamed *Room for Hope*, is centered by an oval-shaped mahogany table seating twenty. The Renaissance paintings that once circled the room have been replaced by the pope's pop-culture favorites: *Peter, Paul, and Mary, the Beatles, Gary Tru...*

"Footnote!!"[9]

Pause.

Seated at one end of the table the pope smiled at his advisors one by one and then lowered his head for the mandatory twenty minutes of quiet prayer.

Time passes. Then raising his head the pope beamed.

"Anyone know why I'm smiling"?

Pause.

"You won the lottery"?

"The Lobos won last night"?

"Because we're faced with an impossible task"?

"Right".

"So we'll have to depend on God's guidance. But..."

"Remember the wheat field"?

Everyone knew the wheat field sermon. As the priest was going on about God sending sunshine and rain to raise wheat, a voice called out, "Not much wheat without a farmer".

"So we have a role to play too. Who wants to start"?

And so for the next two hours Philip listened, condensing the varied responses into three piles. Notify all clergy and parish secretaries to report any signs of exceptional male sanctity. Monitor the media for miracles, and three, attach a tracking device to Schatzi's underbelly to follow her progress. When all three plans were approved Hans raised another concern.

"Security. Surely Lucy and Bells Z are aware of our plans. We need to provide a distraction, and if possible *plant a mole* in their midst".

***

Which leads seamlessly to the Dark Side's response. The Evil Embassy, closed a few pages back, reopened behind closed doors. No sign on the door, no plaque, no house number, but inside things were humming. Lucy and Bells Z were meeting privately while the staff speculated on what lay ahead.

Assassinate Biden? Poison Swiss drinking water? Assassinate Vice-President Harris? A nuclear accident in North Korea? But Lucy and Bells Z walking down a long hall toward a soundproof room modeled on the Fuhrerbunker were pondering a slightly different approach to creating chaos.

Sclummmmm. Closing the fur lined underground oak door gently Bells Z waved Lucy to the chair where Adolf Hitler had once rested his body in the *Fuhrerbunker*. Bells Z was a caped figure six inches taller than the average villain whose face was half hidden under a black slopping hat common in old Fritz Lang film noirs from post WWI Berlin.

"Lucy"?

"Yes mein herr"?

"You've read the report"?

Lucy smiles.

---

[9] Not accepted. No more footnotes. List quotes has been filled until further notice.

"Well"?

"I agree. It's the best option we have".

***

Good guys and bad guys don't often agree but Jerusalem was an easy exception. Where else would one look for Jesus but back in the Holy Land? Bells Z and Lucy Lucifer conferred, agreed; and a week later two rings of informants surrounded the *Church of the Holy Sepulcher* in Jerusalem where Jesus was said to have been left on a heavy wooden cross to die.

And then days later - O my God – Jesus was seen alive: talking and eating with his old friends.[10] From Paul knocked from his blessedhorseblinded to Dr. King, Bishop Tutu, and Mother Teresa hundreds, perhaps thousands, have heard (more likely) or seen (less likely) the risen Jesus. Saint Augustine heard the voice in the garden calling him to a new life. Teresa of Avila met the child Jesus coming down the stairs, a woman I know played duets with Jesus by her side on the piano. Julian of Norwich saw and conversed with Jesus in a series of encounters she wrote of later in *Revelations of Divine Love,* but most Christians encounter Jesus in other ways, as Dorothy Day did in the daily Mass, or as many do in Mother Nature and Father Sky. In music, poetry, or art. So many ways our gracious Lord reaches out to lead us into the good life.

The embrace of creation warms our heart. We got the sun in the morning and the moon at night and we're alright. O praise our gracious Lord. Our *Sovereign Source.* The *Great Mercy.* Our true heart in which we rest when times are hard. Sleepless nights awake with fear or pain. Our waking hours spent brooding on failing faculties, unfriendly neighbors, competitive coworkers, the wrong party in power, fending off cries for help, or giving in to serve those whose agendas interrupt our own. Pouring good will and caring into the restless ocean of human discontent. Grieving for loved ones once close as a phone call. The injustice visited on the housing poor, the food poor, crowded in slums, migrant camps and tent cities on the edge of towering cities where so often, so very often, corruption reigns at the top. And the good life means large houses and low taxes, without the burden of caring for one's neighbor. Paul's "Groaning Creation".

And yet if we welcome the relief of despair we take the despair of those around us into our hearts. That's when we cry out to barren skies for hope, for love, to fill our ravaged hearts that we may wake with a winged heart and give thanks for another day of loving.

Woof.

The outer ring surrounded Jerusalem; the inner ring circled the church itself…

Later. But first the…

***

---

[10] But it didn't stop there. Scripture says 500 saw Jesus alive after his death. Thousands more since claim to have seen or more likely heard Jesus. Many of these are what the bible calls false prophets. "Lord, lord" Christians who claim to; but do not do the will of God. Mt. 7: 21

Woof.

Dr. King, head down on the kitchen table, heard Christ say "Stand up for justice, stand up for truth, stand up for peace and God will be at your side forever".

Tourists in Berne come in all shapes and sizes, so no one was surprised to see a tall cloaked gentleman having black coffee at the Tingle-Kringle outdoor café with a veiled woman in mourning. Speaking in a harsh guttural language the waiter and those seated nearby did not recognize, the couple spoke quietly for perhaps ten minutes and then left the table to go their separate ways.

When the grieving widow and her tall comforter were out of sight their waiter took a bathroom break and cell-phoned Madam President's secretary who immediately rose from her desk and walked to the presidential office across the room. Knock. Knock, knock... knock.

"You got it"? Hannah stood up from behind her imperial desk.

"I got it. Not a language I've ever heard before, but it's all here" and she handed the listening device to her boss, who had the Ork-like conversation translated by a sly-eyed monk in Transylvania. One day short of a week later Madam President met with her trusted advisors in the *Small Mammals Room* at the *Beastly Bottoms*.

***

As Hannah approached the *Small Mammals Room* along the well-lit corridor reserved for media-shy VIPs the racquet grew louder. *What the hell was going on?* Opening the door Hannah saw two burly wait staff and Hans restraining Wigs from reaching the far wall where the hindquarters of one of his beloved dachshunds was mounted on a bronze-colored plaque. This was not the mild-mannered Wigs she'd known. Red faced as a mandrill's rump, eyes wide as a rutting rhino, limbs flailing and kicking, Wigs finally had to be sedated by a conk on the head.

When Wigs revived, back against the wall, blinking and shaking his brains back in place, there was the owner crouched beside him apologizing for the abomination which would be removed immediately.

"And given the burial he deserves in..."

Woof.

"my backyard next to..."

WOOF.

When Wigs had been helped up and the CFJ Stout Lads and several others were seated around a hard glass table on high stools Hannah began.

***

<u>Somewhere over the rainbow way up high</u>

"Several others, Sam"?

"Arnold Really O'Reilly; Norbertines: abbot Joel, Sister Phyllis, and Brother Andrew; the hefty kid from Georgia and his friend Sam Cohen the rabbi's son. And the pope".

***

"Forget the two rings for a minute. First we've got to get Schatzi to Israel. My guess is Bells Z will be expecting her to cross the Atlantic and wend her way across Europe to Jerusalem. Or maybe the Pacific and across Asia".

37

"Too complicated. Why not just wait for Schatzi in Israel? There're a thousand ways to get there, but she has to end up in Jerusalem".

Pause for thoughtful reflection.

"So," Sister Phyllis," your suggestion would be to discuss ways of slipping Schatzi into Israel before she meets Jesus in the *Holy Sepulcher"?*

"Yes".

Pause for reflection.

"Humm".

"Yes young man"?

"Well… why not have Schatzi shipped to Jerusalem by way of… Oslo? Or any place Z won't be expecting".

"Z won't care how she gets in. He'll just check all in-coming flights".

"And

"Why not send a decoy first? Then Schatzi on the next flight"?

"Might work".

"Might not. Too risky".

Pause.

"Bus? Trains? By car? On foot from Jordan or Syria"?

"Again, Z won't care till Schatzi gets to *Jerusalem".*

And so it was agreed Schatzi would be helicoptered in from Cairo; and placed in a JSPCA-HOME until she was taken to the sacred site by abbot Joel who was leading a group of pilgrims through the Holy Land.

CHAPTER 10

WHAT HAPPENED AT THE CHURCH OF THE HOLY SEPULCHER

Huddled against the driving rain just outside the door to the *Chapel of the Apparition* around behind the narrow main entrance to the *Church of the Holy Sepulchre* three workman waited while the chubby fourth workman fumbled to find the keys. But before he could open the door another group of workmen appeared. From then on things moved rapidly as the two groups without a word began pushing, shoving, and punching one another for control of a handheld covered wire cage the first group was defending. Whoa! Suddenly *Chubby's* group backed away from an AK-47 cradled in the arms of a smiling workman.

"Ungrah sucor yahgrissss".

"Uncover the cage".

Uncovered the cage was empty.

Meanwhile Schatzi had slipped through the narrow front entrance to the most convoluted, congested, collection of chapels under one roof in the world. Normally crowded with tourists of every religious or nonreligious persuasion: multi-robed monks and dignitaries from the various Christian denominations from Catholic to Coptic, the church was silent and bare of any living soul. The FJC had done its job well preparing for the encounter between Jesus and the chosen canine. As Schatzi approached the rock which had once blocked the tomb in which Jesus had been laid after his death, and from which he reappeared, vertical after three days, everyone's favorite long dog paused; crouched on the hard tiled floor, lowered her head and stretched her paws toward the tomb. Then moving around the rock, panting in quick short bursts, she closed her eyes as she anticipated meeting her Creator face to face. When she opened her eyes the tomb was empty.

PART III

THE MIDDLE

CHAPTER 11

WHAT NOW?

"I didn't see that coming".

"Caroline?... You knew of course".

"Of course".

Pause.

"So you must know what's coming next"?

"Of course".

"So"?

Silence.

"So unless you get things started again our riveting narrative is over, when the reader can plainly see there's lots more to come".

***

It was a gloomy bunch who met in the *Small Mammals* room. Hannah, the two Bernese Stout Lads, three Norbertines, Hossie Corrie, and the pope. After twenty minutes rehashing what went wrong, replenished by *rosti* (a Swiss potato cake) with apple sauce and beverage, Hans piped up.

"So we start again. Finding Jesus. I suggest we list our responses on yellow pads or electronic devices and compare notes".

"Yellow pads? Electronic devices"?

"Unmentioned in real time; helpful for some in story time".

No one objected and half hour later Hans turned to the pope, who waved him away, and as the others nodded Hans continued.

"Wigs"?

"I've got nothin'. We could check with our Catholic sources, but that only swells the circle of uncertainty".

The little gathering looked up.

"Madam"?

"Yes Heidi"?

"Will there be anything else, Madam President"?

Smiles and head shakes all round and Heidi retreated back into the kitchen.

The three Norbertines also passed and finally Hans turned to Hossie.

"Why not keep our eye out – or is it in? – for signs of exceptional sanctity? We do have Catholic and other friendly sources globally and hopefully, we can *weed out the false alarms* until…"

WOOF? Woof? WOOF?

"When our sacred suspect has been located, Schatzi, you will be dispatched to sniff out if he's the real Jesus".

Pause.

"Anything else"? and when no one responded Wigs prepared to close the meeting when Hossie raised his hand.

"Yes Hossie"?

"We'll be getting a lot of calls"?

"Right".

"Emails, text messages and so on".

Hans nods.

"'Won't we need someone to coordinate all the incoming info? Someone Bells Z and Lucy won't expect".

In the silence that followed a note passed around the table.

<u>There's a bug in Hossie's rosti. Hans, ask again for a contact person. Blessings. P.N.</u>

Short pause.

"What about Arnold"?

And since no one else had any ideas, and it was the pope's suggestion, everyone concurred; the pope said a short prayer and the meeting adjourned.

Later pope Philip met Hannah, passing as a grieving widow in need of papal consolation, in the pope's confessional booth in St. Peters.

"Your Holiness. What was that all about"?

Bob Williams alias Pope Philip Neri broke into a broad grin. Not all of him of course…

"What a meeting! Unbelievable. Hannah we did it".

"Did what"?

Still chortling, bent over with hilarity Bob William finally relaxed, and after several wheezy deep breaths returned to his conversation with Madam President.

"First I made sure Bells Z knew we were meeting. His mole was Heidi the waitress, but when I mentioned excommunication and worse, if she betrayed the Holy Father, she encouraged Bells Z to bug the room".

"How? We checked just before the meeting for bugs in the walls, under the table, in the flowers".

"But not in young Corrie's rosti".

"His what"?

"Potato pancake".

"But Hossie loves food"?

"Ah yes but Hossie was fasting. Mizz Corrie said so when we checked".

Hannah tipped back on the confessional chair.

"You are a crafty dog, your holiness".

Bob Williams smiled.

"Which means", Hannah went on, "Bells Z will be chasing Arnold all over New England while Arnold is on vacation at an undisclosed happy place somewhere in the green-bright forests of northern New Mexico".

"And Heidi devastated over her intended grievous sin, has taken her vows as a Maryknoll sister in the convent in Ossining, New York".

"Where in New York"?

"On the southern tip, next to Sing Sing, across from…"

"Arf".

***

Back in the *Silent Sisters'* underground dungeon Z and Lucy were too engrossed in their own thoughts to notice the bat shit on the dirt floor, or the thin rats cowering in the corner. With his Fritz Lang sloping black hat off Bells Z was a terrifying sight. His fiery eyes glaring from chalky white skin, long black lice-laced hair, and a twisted mouth frozen in contempt for all living creatures, even unsettled Lucy the bewitchingly hard eyed *La Dame Sans Merci*. Even the rats kept their distance.

"Haga depato hissing lepurats. Yah. Yah. SSSsenfrout".

"I don't speak Ork".

"Three weeks. Nothing. Three weeks microfilming the woods from above from Maine to Connecticut. Nothing. Scheibe!"

"Heidi? We could…"

"In a convent. Leave her be. Scheibe!"

There was a long pause while our two villains sat brooding over what had gone wrong. Until. Until a grinchy grin spread across Bells Z's chalky face".

"Look for the weakest link".

Pause.

"Hans. He crossed the line once. Perhaps he will again. Think Lucy. What's his weakest link"?

"A challenge. Something to engage his restless brain".

Pause.

"And loyalty. Loyalty to what he believes is the right thing to do".

Pause.

"Apart from Hannah and her friends".

"Something he can bring to them as a *fact accomplee*".

***

Sky Wideeye whom we haven't heard from in awhile was not in a good mood. Profits from *Sky-Hans Incorporated* were non-existent. They'd had their fifteen minutes of fame. Sky having spent his pile on the *Get High with Sky, a fly* by night affair which the *Las Vegas Sun* referred to as "Party Time Plus" was broke. Hans, who'd invested heavily in a startup travel agency that advertised "We put the You in Ukraine '' was also broke. In short Hans was looking for ways to recoup his losses and, when

Sky called to say he'd gotten some money from a hopped-up greyhound, would Hans be interested in meeting in his apartment close by the old Zytglosse Hans agreed.

"If I'm late I'll leave the door unlocked".

***

No sooner had Hannah's savvy Stout Lad entered Sky's ransacked apartment than two burly polizei appeared and cuffed him. A half hour later poor Hans found himself downtown being sentenced to two years for entering and breaking without…

Arf.

***

"Sam"?

"Ummm"?.

"A bit too condensed? Two sentences and poor Hans walks into a friend's apartment and finds himself in jail for two years".

"Ok. I'll check with Caroline and try again".

***

"Thanks".

Pause.

Hans looked across the wobbly round topped table in the *Dee Zertz* ice cream parlor at an attractive woman in her mid-fifties.

"But what led you to post my bail"?

"I was a friend of your late mother. My name's Hilda Zozentot".

After Hilda is uncomfortably seated on a long-legged tall chair Hans and Hilda look at the worn and weary elderly blond waitress wearing a perky white hat with Dee printed on one side and Zertz on the other who is resting on one foot waiting to take their order.

Hilda smiled weakly as people will when they're about to reject the expectations of others.

"Can you come back in five minutes? Your eighty item menu…"

"Excuse me Hilda. I recommend the Louberry Strudel and a Swiss coke".

"Two please" and Hans turned to the work at hand. Twenty minutes later Hilda excused herself for an early dinner with her husband, a retired Jungfrau mountain guide, while Hans lingered over a sugar-loaded Swiss cappuccino and skimmed a dozen or so Catholic publications for news of unidentified male sanctity.

Later Hilda Zozentot cell-phones Bells Z.

"Hans is broke and looking for work. I sense he's not as particular as he might be. He's not only broke he's in debt".

Bells Z's grim face morphed into a Grinchy grin as he leaned over and whispered to Lucy.

"We've got hm".

"Hilda"?

"Still here".

"Who's he in debt to"?

Hilda began to read the list till Lucy broke in.

"Just the top two".

"Fast Cash and *Dough to Go"*.

"Thanks Hilda. Catch ya later. And Oh. Why doesn't Hans ask Hannah for help"?

"Too proud".

***

You've reached the residence of Hans Yodelgruber. Please leave….

Click. Pause.

"Mr. Yodelgruber this is Larry Liftoff of *Alpine Electronics"*.

"Yes"?

"Have you read the email we sent"?

"Yes I have".

"And do you wish to discuss our proposal in person"?

"Affirmative".

"You will be contacted in the near future. Thank you for offering your services to Alpine Electronics".

Three days later Hans had discussed and accepted…

WOOF! ARF! GRRRR.!

Confusion reigns. Voices from everywhere interrupt one another. The characters revolt. Hannah is tired of… the pope resigns… the Stout Lads come to fisticuffs… the Norbertines reconvert to… Hossie loses weight to join the rodeo wrestling wild buffalo…

"Buffalo aren't…"

"Who cares. It's a mess, a hubbub, a hullabaloo".

"A hubbub *is* a hullabaloo".

Finally things settle. The revolt is over and the cowed characters agree to put their grievances to one side to refocus on the task at hand. Finding Jesus. But not all.

***

"Schatzi's right. This story line is going nowhere. Hans too proud to ask for help? No one checks on Hilda's background? I like Larry Liftoff but space travel takes us magna-miles away from our gritty down to earth light-hearted dead serious theological mystery. Finding Jesus. Sam"?

"Ummm".

"Any thoughts"?

"Ask Caroline".

"She knows but she won't tell".

Bark! Bark! BARK!! Yap-yap-yap. Grrrr.

"Schatzi says to let her loose and she'll lead us to Jesus".

"Let her loose where"?

Woof…. Woof…. Woof… Yap-arf.

"Albuquerque"?

And so when Hossie Corrie's grandparents Betty and John moved into their first floor dog-world apartment in *La Vida Llena* Schatzi was with them.

"Charly"?

"Yes"?

"You speak Spanish".

"*La Vida Llena* means *The Full Life*".

"In their 90's? Their full life was fifty years ago".

"How old are you Sam"?

"Timeless. I'm just a fleeting image in our illustrious author's boney skull"?

"Stay in character then. You're in your forties. The full life isn't full till it's over. *'Youth sees but half. See all nor be afraid'*. Browning. The full life embraces the ailments of age. Every creaky joint, every pause for words that don't come, every cathing, hopeful the urethra hasn't narrowed enough to send the old man back to the urine bag strapped to his leg by day, hung overhead at night, which hopefully won't overflow as it once did when…"

Bowow… Arf… Woof.

"But also every new day out the window bright with beauty. A daily *To Do* list where family, friends, writing, and medical appointments compete for attention. Which reminds me".

"Of what"?

"Beautiful women".

Woof?

"Women with wrinkles. Women who have the full life etched on their bodies. Stretch marks, sagging breasts and bottoms, dark flesh under their bright eyes, who walk with canes, or walkers, or sit in wheelchairs to be pushed by aids or aging spouses. Women whose minds are filled with memories that come and go. Women honored by their children, and friends who lower their voices and speak slowly. Women on the edge of eternity waiting to be taken way up high where dreams that they dare to dream really do come true.

***

"Sam".

Nods.

"Have you noticed that some sentences demand a response, while others are conversation stoppers followed by an awkward silence? Other silences change the direction of the conversation without a word being said".

"Jesus walked this lonesome valley. Nobody else could walk it for him. He had to walk it by himself…

We must walk this lonesome valley. We have to walk it by ourselves. Nobody else can walk it for us. We have to walk…"

CHAPTER 12

ALBUQUERQUE PLUS

For Betty and John Corrie *La Vida Llena, Albuquerque,* New Mexico's only in-house life care retirement community, has been an adventure. The first six months the livin' was easy. Sleep late, no cooking, no dishes, no laundry, free movies, lectures, and eight resident-run, management-supported, activity groups including Current Events, Penny Ante Poker, Classic Films, Dr. King's Life and Legacy, Quilting, Art History, and How to Write Poetry, with or without reason and rhyme. Living in *Independent Living* Betty and John made new friends. The last friends they'd make in this life.

"In this life"?

"John's a Christian. Betty's had a guardian angel since she was five. Heaven's part of the package along with serving the poor, peace work, prayer, and a viable faith community".

"What kind of Christian? Lots to choose from. 41,000 independent denominations. *Evangelical? Mainstream? Liberal? Peacenik Quaker, Mennonite, Church of the Brethren.* Conservative, traditional Pope John Paul II or liberal, popes John XXIII and Francis; the *USCCB, The United States Council of Catholic Bishops* or Dorothy Day and the *Catholic Worker".*

"And John"?

"Two. Plain and fancy. John was raised a Quaker, joined Friends in his mid-twenties, and became a Catholic when he was in his early…"

Woof? Arf? Woof?

"forties. *Mass* on Saturday. *Friend's Meeting* on Sunday. After Betty fell, sitting back against the wall in the bathroom between the tub and the toilet reaching out with her big toe to the opposite wall for the pull cord, the Corries moved to *Assisted Living".*

Woof?... Woof?.... Woof?

After a month, while Betty was rehabbing and John and two friends had spent three days assembling a blond oak bureau and matching desk which looks out the window onto a leafy courtyard while John writes, Schatzi was released to find Jesus in Santa Fe.

***

Meanwhile Hans was starting his new job as a special consultant with *Alpine Electronics,* a mega corporation servicing the NASA space program, and less publicly the listening device industry. His first meeting with his boss Larry Liftoff went well. In addition to writing promotional material for the media, Hans would be a listening device inspector separating experimental listening devices into three piles: Market ready, Needs work, and Discard.

Three weeks later Hans received a small package from *Sender Unknown* he knew to be Hannah, containing a bug disguised as a Timex watch. Tuning into the watch Hannah heard an Ork-like voice telling Larry Liftoff **Garf sin yaaah Ahattswit zelrlt freg het unfragen xert hat,** translated by the sly-eyed monk in Transylvania into English as "The dog's in Albuquerque heading for Santa Fe. Terminate dog".

***

Smooosh. The fur lined oak door to the Small Mammals room closed slowly on Hannah, Wigs, Hans, and the pope in jogging sweats, who were seated on tall stools around a hard glass table waiting to order.

Pause.

"Double espresso".

"Cappuccino".

"Two Swiss Cokes".

"And fondue for four".

Another pause as the four friends took time to reacquaint themselves with signs of change in each others facial features. Hans looking at...

Woof.

"Morning lads. And *Your Holiness.* The news is Schatzi needs to be in *St. Francis* [Cathedral] in Santa Fe to meet Father Jay Clarke, who has a few leads on finding Jesus. The problem is Bells Z and Lucy also know the dog will be going to Santa Fe".

"We could leak the news that the dog's going to Las Cruces on her way to Carlsbad Caverns".

And so a few days later while Bells Z and Lucy were waiting outside the elevator on the ground floor at the Caverns, Shatzi was leaping, yipping and licking Father Jay's russet-red bearded face in the small chapel just off the main sanctuary in St. Francis Cathedral, a block off the Plaza in Santa Fe.

Woof? Arf?......bow wow?... ???

"I'll tell you after Mass".

***

Known as *Critters' Mass* to celebrate saint Francis's love for all living creatures the sanctuary was packed with dogs and cats, a few parakeets, goldfish, hamsters, pigs, a horse or two, and a semi-circle of donkeys who were given the place of honor in front of the altar. What a joyous hullabaloo. What a joyful noise unto the Lord, until Father Rohr raised his hands and the congregation fell silent. Lowering his head Father Rohr prayed that the gift of tongues might bless the animals with English in order to understand the sermon. Then lifting his head as tears ran down his cheeks Father Rohr opened his heart to the critters he loved.

"Dear friends I must begin by begging your forgiveness for the atrocities my species has visited on you and your families. The little ones cuddled against their mothers...

"Hold on now. That's a bit much".

"… That critters have no feelings? That they do not care for and cuddle their young as we do? We have cut down their forests and paved over the meadows. We have poisoned the rivers, lakes, and oceans with oily gunk. Most grievously we have butchered the defenseless smaller critters: noisily clucking chickens, squawking turkeys, and netful after netful of fish, shrimp, and other ocean delicacies. The peaceful cattle and lumbering buffalo. The defenseless sheep. Any edible critter ends up lifeless on the plates of the hungry master race".

Again, the assistant pastor, a young man whose family raised cattle in Texas, interrupted until a neighboring rattler slithered up his inside pant leg, and he had to leave, hobbling his way to the ER. When things settled down again Father Rohr turned the corner to the hopeful side of his sermon.

"Yet despite the atrocities my race has inflicted on you, you have enriched our lives in so many, many ways. Soaring above us: dipping, wheeling, and gliding in thin air; beating your wings through angry winds; twittering and singing in the trees around us. You have…"

Woof. Woof.

"Just one real bird"?

Arf.

"The wide-winged skimmer, black on top, belly-white, moves motionless inches above the still bay-water for half a mile; her bright red bill trolling for sun-seeking lesser life venturing close to the surface. Whales and wailing wallabies, penguins and white mountain panthers; a thousand, thousand, circling critters live on the edge of our finance-focused lives of quiet desperation. Offering their healing presence".

Father Rohr paused, took a deep breath and concluded his sermon with words from scripture.

"*Then God said, 'Let the earth bring forth critters of every kind: cattle and creeping things and wild critters of the earth of every kind. And it was so. And God saw that it was good…'* Rejoice dear friends and be glad. Your Creator welcomes you into the land of milk and honey" and as Father Rohr spread his arms wide the assorted sounds of critter world filled *Saint Francis Cathedral.*

***

"Sam? What's wrong"?

"Nothing's wrong".

Pause.

More pause.

"Side trips, Charly. Our riveting narrative has deteriorated into nothing but side trips".

"Sam, don't worry. We'll get there. Wherever there is".

"We had an outline…"

Pause.

"A tacit agreement. Unspoken agreements aren't binding".

"Mysteries don't wander. Where's Jesus? That's our mystery. Novels can wander, plays can wander. Sagas like *Canterbury Tales* can wander. Take out one or two tales and others fill in, but mysteries build suspense. Except for standard interludes like food and sex every chapter builds on the one before. Wandering's a distraction. Mysteries are like short stories. Every sentence…"

"Maybe it's not a mystery".

"Finding Jesus? Good guys and bad guys. That's a mystery".

Pause.

"Charly"?

"What"?

"No murder. No body in the library or washed ashore on the Thames. There was no murder".

"Jesus was murdered".

"Two thousand years ago".

"And today"?

***

After Mass Shatzi and Father Jay met in the little chapel off to the right. Fifteen saints and Jesus painted on a wooden plank on the far wall mingled with the prayers of those sitting in front while Shatzi and Father Jay whispered in the back. Fifteen minutes later Father Jay rose from the hard oak bench, blessed Shatzi with the sign of the cross, stroked her furry skull and turned to leave.

Woofwoofarf… arfarfarfarf woof… bowwow arf woof.

Father Jay sat down and listened to Shatzi' low staccato growling, until the hearty, russet-red bearded priest understood. Three options. Jerusalem, tent city outside Rio de Janeiro, and an Irish bar in Philly.

***

Jerusalem.

Sitting alone apart from his small group of pilgrim-tourists gathered in front of the *Garden of Gethsemane* Pastor Jones[11] smiled to himself thinking what a difference a year makes. *Last May I was…*

Woof.

Only ten after the two cancellations, but it's been a good group. Attentive; and they seem to get on well together. Sensing his flock were becoming restless – forget the becoming, they were restless - Pastor Jones stood up, shivered his shoulders, and stepped back into the group.

"Good question Ailene but no, the thick-trunked olive tree in front of us is not the original, but somewhere among the ancestral trees at the base of the Mount of Olives our Lord had his down time". After two more questions, a rereading of the relevant biblical passage, and an extended discussion on human suffering Pastor Jones, "just call me Bill" but no one did, encouraged the pilgrims to reflect on their own moments of misery. Finally after a few minutes of quiet prayer the group moved on, while nearby a young Palestinian mother, with her sleeping toddler beside her, wept quietly over the loss of her parents and the misery of her people.

Tent City near Rio De Janeiro
Associated Press July 1, 2021

People carry their belongings after they were evicted from land designated for Petrobras [the state-run oil refinery], *at a settlement coined the "First of May Refugee Camp" named for the date people moved in setting up tents and shacks in Itaquai, not far from Rio De Janeiro.*

---

[11] Pastor Jones, designated villain of *Bang!* one and two, was shown the wickedness of his ways toward the end of *Bang!Bang!*.

Televised images showed residents blocking the entrance to the campsite with bonfires as police launched tear gas canisters and fired water cannons at the tents.

Rio's police department said eviction was part of a legal...

Woof!

Petrobras said the company had provided hand sanitizers and face masks and offered transportation to the nearest bus station.

One unidentified woman appeared on Globo television begging for help. "I'm a domestic worker" she said through tears, "The woman fired me because of the pandemic. Help me please: I have nowhere to go. I don't have any family".

***

"Sam"?

"Yes Charly"?

"We're commentators. Right"?

"We're like Greek Gods far above the shifting tides of conflict, war, and reconciliation".

"Right".

"And yet Sam my heart weeps for the Palestinian mother, and her soul-sister without a family in Brazil".

Pause as Charly and Sam reflect on their abandoned sisters and brothers, until Sam lifted his tear-stained face.

"And Jesus? Where was Jesus? Where *is* Jesus? Praying for us from Heaven while we lift our arms pleading for help here on earth? Christians preach about their wonderful Savior, Shepherd, Friend, God incarnate whatever that means, Creator, Lord of Heaven and earth, who left us on our own several millennium ago"?

Long pause.

"Sam"?

Nods.

"Remember the picture where figures morph into another image"?

"Diptych"?

"A white tree in the center and if you look twice, two women in the dark background".

"Except in our diptych if you look closely the two women are embraced by the figure of a first century Galilean healer".

"And some people see one image, while others see two".

"Interesting observation Charly but it doesn't answer my question. Where is Jesus today? Still stuck in Heaven, afraid to return after the unruly reception he received the first time"?

***

McGillin's Olde Ale House, Philadelphia

Bars during drinking hours are crowded. And so's McMillin's, but McMillin's has several distinctive features other bars don't. First it is olde, the oldest in the city. Opened in 1860 by Irish immigrants' "Pa" and "Ma" McMillian and run by McMillians for two years short of a century until 1958 when their daughter, one of thirteen, sold McMillian's to its present owner. Known as "Bell in Hand" for the ship's bell kept behind the counter, which is still rung to celebrate large tips, and whenever one of the five local sports team scores.[12] Keeping things real, bad karaoke singers are gonged and booed.

McMillin's is also known as a political bar where local politicians meet to be seen drinking one of Philly's thirty-five local brews. And so we come to mayor Goodenough, a roly-poly good-natured hugger, who leaves most of the office work to underlings while he meets and greets his beloved constituents.

***

***

                        ***

"Charly"?

"Yes Sam".

"That's it? That's Jesus on earth today? I understand a Palestinian mother grieving her people's plight. Driven from their homeland. Deprived of their dignity. And the homeless Brazilian domestic worker without family. I understand Jesus lives among the poor, but a well-off politician"?

"If, as Quakers say, there's that of God in every…"

"But most people aren't Quakers".

"No. But *John's* gospel says the same thing. Right at the beginning. *"All things came into being through him (Jesus)*[13] *and without him (Jesus) not one thing came into being. What has come into being was life and that life was the light of all people"*. In other words God, Jesus, Life, and Light refer to the same spiritual presence which is in each one of us".

"But I don't…"

"Doesn't matter if we know it or not. Physically I don't know all the 7,500 parts of my body, but that doesn't interfere with my living".

"So a spiritual component is in each one of us, whether we know it or not? Even a roly-poly politician"?

"Right".

"Hum. But that's not all that's in us is it"?

"Sadly no. The rest of the quote *The light shines in the darkness and the darkness did not overcome it* sounds hopeful but that's in God's other world. Here on earth who knows what evil lurks in the hearts of every human being"?

                        ***

"Charly"?

"Hum".

"About our last conversation".

"Is there a problem? I thought we were on the same page, two peas in a pod, paddling the same canoe".[14]

---

[12] Phillies baseball, Eagles football, Sixers basketball, Flyers hockey, and more recently Philadelphia United soccer.

[13] I could have used Christ or Christ Jesus in place of Jesus, but my own experience has focused on the name Jesus.

[14] … Two minds with but a single thought. Two of a kind. Spitting image of… carbon copies, dead ringers, like father like son, cut from the same cloth, mirror images, tarred with the same brush… Woof! … chip off the old… WOOF!

"It's not that, but I'd like to know how the Light that shines in darkness translates outside Christianity? What about Jews? Buddhists? Mother Earth, Father Sky Indians"?

"They have their own language games.[15] Their own way of expressing their fears and aspirations. Buddhists speak of *Nirvana*. Primal peoples in Australia, Africa and around the world use a variety of critter names for the *Divine Dimension* that comes at the end of very long week".

"Charly, are you saying it's all terminology? That different faith communities are all focused on the same mysterious Radiant Goodness, the same Higher Power addressed by many names"?

"Yes and no. Yes we use different words for the source of our longing but no. We…"

"No? Why no? One mountain, one summit. Different terminology, that's all".

"It's the path we take up the mountain that's my immediate concern. I want a Buddhist who believes in the tenets of her faith. A Muslim who bows his head on the hard tile floor praising Allah, the Merciful, the Compassionate; a Jew who wails at the Wall and wears the Yamaha. I want believers who join with comrades and kin on their way through the fiend infested forests to the clearing above the timber line. And the independent loners who would find their own way to the blessedness we all seek. The goal's the same; our paths to the top will vary".

---

[15] Ludwig Wittgenstein's Language Games are the little languages faith communities, political parties, recreation groups etc. use to communicate within the group. Christians use a common language but also a specialized language suited to the history and needs of individual faith communities. Doctors and lawyers use….
Woof. Arf. Woof.

CHAPTER 13

CHARLY'S CRABBY, HANS' SEARCH FOR HAPPINESS, BELLS Z'S HELLHOLE, AND THE ENCHANTED CHALET

"Charly"?

"I'm working. Can we talk later"?

"I've been wondering".

"I said I was working dammit".

"Sorry".

Pause.

"What's wrong Charly? You've been like this for a week now".

"Like what"?

"Distracted. Crabby".

"Aaaaah. Shit…. Shit. Shit. Shit".

"Charly"?

"What is it now"?

Pause.

"I don't know. I'm mad at something but I don't know what".

Pause.

"You know me Sam. Whatta you think"?

Pause.

The two old friends sit quietly until Charly grinds his teeth and a voice he can't keep out takes over. His eyes gleam as the voice screams inner obscenities unheard by Sam. Gradually Charly's face relaxes, and he blinks as if waking from an unsettling dream.

***

Silent Sisters monastery was abuzz with activity welcoming their illustrious leaders home from abroad. But despite a fresh flock of bats, spooky spirits, and a festive banquet of chopped lizards on a bed of lice, Bells Z and Lucy Lucifer didn't look happy. The sisters kept their distance until a select group of seven were called to a meeting in the devil's dungeon.

Looming over his cowed underlings Bells Z's black cape embroidered with sinister incantations, and his blood red evil eyes, gleaming from his pasty white face inspired fear that alerted them to the consequences of deviating from the master's will. Fear mixed with a tinge of curiosity riveted their attention on the two evil ones facing them in the devil's dark dungeon.

Hash gragul dishep die shiest Hans gah nark fuckwet. Slep yah die yah ungrap dsend.

For those who didn't speak Ork Lucy translated.

"Find Hans Yodelgruber and turn him to our intent".

Yahshit volcart krigsot lagassa Hans shesptax loggani fuct da zalla mein sheart.

Again Lucy translated.

"Hans is crafty clever. He sees what others miss. Sadly for us his Swiss heart beats for the uncrowned queen and country. Hans is a man of many moods. No one's quite sure what his weaknesses are".

And so the seven women ranging in temperament, features, and age from their early twenties to their late forties were dismissed to ponder the challenge of matching wits with Madam President's ardent advisor.

***

Having broken with his longtime girlfriend Hans was browsing the *Hot to Trot* dating site when he came upon the promo for Heidi Cowbell. *Mid twenties. Swiss. Likes crossword puzzles, Russian novels, the English journal The Guardian, mountain climbing, and café life. A feminist who likes her privacy. Campaigned for Madam President Hossenhoeffer.* Photo: five foot seven, fetching figure, blond pigtails, carrying a copy of Louise Penny's latest mystery. In short, just the sort of woman Hans was looking for. An attractive, intellectual Switzer.

Hans responded. They met indoors at the *Tingle-Kringle*, got on well, and two weeks later Heidi moved in with Hans. Three weeks later Heidi moved out. Madam President Hossenhoeffer, always suspicious of any outside contacts which, or who, might distract the Stout Lads from their appointed roles as queen Hannah's knights of the coffee table, had checked to discover Heidi had campaigned for Madam President only a week before the election and had previously voted for Hannah's right-wing opponents.

***

The Heritage Room of the Berne Public Library, a narrow room walled by olde newspapers, canton court records, photos and memorabilia of bye-gone days, was one of Hans's happier haunts. Libby the librarian was an old girlfriend who'd co-authored their controversial article, *The Effect of the Alps on the Swiss Psyche*, which was rejected by The *Swiss Journal of Geosciences,* but published in *Blick (Look, Peek)* a popular daily tabloid. The claims that Swiss males struggling to breath thin alpine air sired skinny kids, while others raised on Toggenburg goat's milk were as rammy as…

Woof. Arf. Woof.

Another of Hans and Libby's controversial claims was that Switzers living in lowland cities and towns were brunettes while those on the mountain slopes, closer to the sun, were what became known as solar sisters or sun-blonds.

***

Arf arf arf.

Pause.

"Hans Yodelgruber Hossenfass"?

Hans looked up, stood, and bowed slightly to the attractive middle-aged woman in front of him.

"At your service".

The woman smiled and held out her hand. Hans smiled back and they shook hands.

"My name is Violet von Vittles. I'm the food reporter for station RTS 2. We're doing a series on how food affects one's personal, and even one's working life. I wonder if you'd mind sharing how your taste in food and drink has affected your life"?

And so began another short chapter in Hans Hossenfass's lively life.

"Please be seated".

When Hans and Violet were well seated, had smiled the observing smile one uses in meeting a stranger for the first time…

Woof.

Well of course. How else would one meet someone for the first time but as a stranger?

"Not necessarily. One might well have heard of the person in question for years before ever meeting them".

Picky quibbles aside when Hans and Violet were well seated sipping cappuccino Hans shared his food favorites while Violet recorded his answers on the latest electronic device.

"I eat three meals a day. First a hefty hearty healthy breakfast at the Tingle-Kringle café. I start with a double espresso followed by either Swiss muesli and fruit, or an American breakfast of three eggs over easy on whole wheat toast, three slices of bacon, one sausage, and a blueberry Danish on the weekend. Breakfast sets my still sleepy senses humming with excitement to face the demands, doubts and delights of the new day".

"And lunch"?

"White wine and a sandwich. Swiss on rye. No ham".

"Where"?

"Often with Madam President and Wigs at *Beastly Bottoms*".

Violet and Hans smile.

"Wigs"?

"Ludwig Schlossenmeir Bedfellows, my best friend… Just enough to ease me into the afternoon without feeling as stuffed as…".

"And dinner"?

"Varies. The big meal is breakfast".

After a short conversation in which Violet learned that Hans's parents and his twin sisters still lived in….

Woof.

And Hans learned that Violet, up until she was…

WOOF!

One thing and another Hans accepted Violet's invitation to a homecooked meal in Violet's apartment close by the olde clock tower. Given his choice Hans favored *Veau a la Zurichoise*, sliced veal with mushrooms, paired with a bottle of Swiss Riesling X Sylvaner. Arriving fashionably a few minutes late Hans smiled, kissed Violet on both cheeks, and entered what seemed to Hans a shabby replica of Louie the 14th's decadent French court. Faded curtains, ornate but well-worn high-back chairs, and cheap Fragonard reproductions. Still one must admire the taste that reaches for elegance in restricted circumstance. The meal itself unfortunately for Hans was not memorable; largely because he couldn't remember anything after the first sip of wine.

***

Walking alone on his way to *Beasty Bistro* for lunch with madam president and the other Stout Lads Wiggy Shossenmeir-Bedfellow was admiring the medieval charm of olde Berne when an elderly gentleman stopped and asked if Wiggy might shield him against a strong March breeze while he lit his pipe. As Wigs crouched around the old gentleman he felt a conk on the head and a sharp pain in his side as he was hustled into a black limousine.

Meanwhile hale and hearty Hannah, sitting alone in the *Small Mammals* room, was about to call Wigs and Hans, when two new waiters approached her table and asked if there was anything wrong with her succulent salmon. As she bent over to sniff the pink fish she too was conked on the noggin, a furry black bag slid over her head, and her limp body was lugged out the door to the hallway leading to the kitchen. But instead of the kitchen the two waiters slipped out the service entrance, dumped Hannah in an unmarked black VW Tiguan and slowly eased their way into Berne's mid-day traffic and headed north toward the mountains.

***

Lullaby Land

"Ummmmmm".

"Ummmmmm what"?

"It's not going well below Sam. Hannah's crew's been kidnapped and driven to Bells Z's mountain lair".

"And"?

"And us too. At least for me".

"Us too what"?

"Not going well".

"Why not? At least we're not in Bells Z's rocky hellhole".

"Remember that inner anger I spoke of? That grin and grind wicked smile that took over my face"?

"Yes".

"That's troubling Sam. It means Satan's at work in the cosmic commentators, at least in me, as well as in Hannah's crowd below".

"Satan? Who mentioned Satan"?

***

There was no moat, no stone walls, no turrets, no underground dungeons. No Iron Maidens, no racks, no torture devices of any kind. No evil gnomes roaming the narrow stone passageways of a dank and dreary medieval castle. Rather, secluded on the far north side of the Jungfrau from Berne, one comes upon a large Swiss chalet, *Dreams Come True*, and a barn with Swiss Brown Cows grazing on a green and gently sloping pasture.

Inside the chalet one is met by a receptionist whose appearance varies to meet the expectations of the entering guest. To those of a hearty nature the chalet is a hunting lodge. An Army barracks. A newsroom or television studio. A congressional caucus. To more reflective souls the chalet is a library, classroom, or Zoom room to converse with colleagues around the globe. To scientists a laboratory; to doctors a hospital, to…

Wooof.

And for males with more ordinary ambitions a pool hall, hockey rink, or ethnic meeting place: church, club, or bar. For women a hair salon, shopping mall, a book club, or café for meeting one's friends. In short the chalet is designed to meet the aspirations of every guest who comes in. But never comes out.

CHAPTER 14

HANNAH'S FIRST LOVE. CEREBERUS, THE HAIRY THREE HEADED HOUND. AND SPREADING THE GOOD WOOF

When Hannah and her two Stout Lads woke next morning, they soon found themselves seated outdoors at the Tingle-Kringle café beside a diversely perceived figure.

To Hannah the russet-red bearded young man with bright eyes reminded her of Robbie Burns the Scotch poet from across the border in Dumfries. To Wigs he was an old pal from his summer days in the forest service, and to Hans the figure was Cerberus, the three headed dog who guards the gate to the land of the dead.

"Madam President may we start with you"?

Hannah smiled, ordered a second cup of coffee au laid, waved the question aside, and inwardly drifted into the specifics of her sexual awakening. She was sitting beside Tarry O'Connor on that sunny day beside the river Nith, when Tarry recited Robbie Burn's

> O my Luve is like a red, red rose
>   That's newly newly sprung in June.
> O my Luve is like the melody
>   That's sweetly played in tune.
>
> So fair art thou, my bonnie lass;
>   So deep in luve am I;
> And I will luve thee still, my dear
>   Till a' the seas gang dry.
>
> Till a' the seas gang dry, my dear;
>   And the rocks melt wi' the sun;
> I will luve thee still,
>   While the sands o' life shall run…

Tarry was a strange lad; nervous, shy, romantic; only two years out of puberty. Sitting side by side on the banks of the Nith river, that ran down from Dumfries to Yorkshire, in early June, the first kiss was awkward as most of Tarry's mouth landed on Hannah's cheek. And while she blushed when his hand brushed her blouse she smiled, and the hand kept moving. As affectionate words moved back and forth their breathing shortened, and when he asked permission she whispered "take your time Tarry". Lying under the warm sun listening to the passing river, belly to belly, her loins moved slowly on their own as Tarry-No-Longer's penis pressed past her fuzzy soft lower lips into the sacred sanctuary of love that brought smiles to the angels on high.

"O my love, my darling boy. Tarry no longer... Hannah. SweetHannah, mybonnielass. My darling, I... O O O. *Faster, faster. OmyGod... OmyGod faster... Yes Tarry. Yes. Yes, OGod yes".*

Hannah smiled remembering the long hour talking quietly on the other side of intimacy, gazing into the soft face that had inspired her first passion, until warm afternoon melded into cool early evening. And as the sun slipped from view to warm other worlds the young lovers packed the wicker basket, folded the blanket, and headed back to Dumfries.

***

"Ludwig Schossenmeir"?

"Heinrich! Heinrich Hepplehardenstein Von Gruber! What a surprise. I'm dumbfounded. After, what is it? Ten years"?

***

Meanwhile Hans was facing the three hairy-headed Cerberus, the horrifying hell hound from the underworld who guards the dear departed from escaping back into our world, steps back. He'd always liked dogs: loyal, protective...

Schatzi growled. "Grrrr. Snarl. Gr..." but froze when Cerberus lunged forward, eyes blazing, roared back **"Urah...yah hess ssss schlata. lata. Raa. Snapt snizzin Gar Gar Gar Dy Dy Dy!!!"**

Seeing Cereberus had stopped short Hans held out his hands palms up, as he looked down unable to hold his gaze on the three snarling heads and waited for Schatzi's translation.

"Ruff. Ruff... Cerebrums says he's a guard dog not an attack dog. He says we're to go back to our own people. Woof".

"Ask him why he has three heads".

Pause while the two, or is it four, dogs talked together.

Ruff... woof, **arrrrah,** yip, **arrah, yip**. Pip.... Nez....Nargar.... **hellut** .... Nezzz. Holop".

"The first head says Stay Back; the second growls Ork-like incantations, and the third head's eyes spits sparks into anyone foolish enough to return his gaze".

***

Meanwhile Charly and Sam looking down on our riveting narrative are bewildered. What has an enchanted chalet got to do with the search for Jesus?

"Charly"?

"I'm not sure what's going on. I know what's happening. We're in a haunted house with a thousand rooms that so far have nothing to do with the search for Jesus. There's the obligatory sex scene; a three-headed wild-eyed mythical canine; and Wiggy meets an old friend. Caroline"?.

"Go back to Hannah's crew imprisoned in Bells Z's dark dungeon".

***

"Why," thought Hannah chained in darkness to a nearby iron bedpost, *"am I still alive? What is it they want from me"?* Staring into space Hannah smiled. *They can take away the world around me but the world within my bony skull is beyond their reach.* Waiting had never been easy for Switzerland's first lady, but Hannah was used to facing her daily duties and doubts head on, and if waiting was the obvious option Hannah amused herself with the sweet scent of memorable moments. Holding mum's hand walking through snow to the warm church on Christmas eve; picking blueberries with dad in Scotland just across the border. Reading Jules Verne's *Around the World in 80 Days*, into a wider world. Snuggling with Tarry-No-Longer. Guinness and salty finger food at the Beastly…. "**Hannah Hossenhoeffer. Come with us**".

Led by two pasty-faced Neanderthals clad in black leather down dank dungeon passageways Hannah soon found herself in a dimly lit, feces-foul smelling, interrogation room seated beside Hans and Wiggy in front of the Wicked White Warlock with piercing red eyes. After a short pause Bells Z explained that Hannah's two parents and a "Scotch bedfellow" were under surveillance, and that Hans and Wiggy's family likewise were being monitored with an option to kill "Unless our little talk goes well".

The little talk of course focused on Hannah persuading the good guys from Pope Philip on down to Hossie Corrie to call off the search for Jesus.

Silence.

"We'll need time alone to discuss your offer".

"I'll be back in fifteen minutes".

When Bells Z returned Hannah agreed, called the pope, explained the situation, and waited two days until the Vatican confirmed that the search for Jesus had been called off. Forced by the terms of their reversible agreement Hannah and the lads were then released. Which left an obscure low bellied long dog, who was not part of the agreement, to take up the torch for jus….

Woof.

***

While things have come to a standstill in our riveting narrative on earth, things weren't aren't going any better above where Charly and Sam, two of our cosmic commentors, are having their own problems. Namely Charly's mindless rage inwardly screaming obscenities whenever the search for Jesus is alluded to.

"I can't help it, Sam. I try but…"

Woof.

"Caroline what's going on"?

"Don't fight it Charly. It's not your war".

"I thought we were beyond the tensions and terrors that plague our friends below".

"Obviously we're not. The war goes on even in our realm".

"Between"?

"Radical Evil and Radiant Goodness".

Pause.

Cough.

Long pause.

"Even in you? But you're the…"

"Especially in me Charly. I'm the devil's first enemy".

***

What's needed here is a comment on the commentators' conundrum. Is the author implying that Caroline, who's you know who, still struggling to do the right thing?

Of course not. If God isn't good as is, it's a whole new game. But God is good; radiantly good, gloriously good, good beyond anything us poor human beings can imagine. God, and that of God in each of us, thinks well of others, forgives others, and enjoys coffee and croissant with others. The difference is God is good, while the rest of us are aspiring to be good. We all have an inclination to evil; but thank God we also…

Woof.

Meanwhile Schatzi was barking, yapping, woofing, the news that the fate of the long-legged feeders with soft hands and bad breath was now in the hands of dog world. Find Jesus! But where to start? Dogs were of course all over. Too many to contact. What Schatzi needed was a canine committee to organize the search. Which brought her to the annual *Westminster Kennel Club Dog Show* in Madison Square Garden where, when she appeared in the front row with her American owner Arnold Really O'Reilly, she *caught the eye* (yuck!) of a sennenhund (a Bernese Swiss farm dog) currently in second place in the hound group, who barked back he'd slip his leash after BIS (Best in Show) was over and meet Schatzi in Central Park. Tossed out of the Garden for barking, Schatzi (and Arnold) took the tube downtown to the bowery where the *Marvelous Mutts* (the *Mixed Breeds Dog Shows of America*) were holding *their* annual event. After enlisting a dachshund-shih tzu, and several Heinz 57 mutts whose unrecorded ancestry remains - well unrecorded, it was agreed to meet uptown by the little-known Blue Banshee Bridge in Central Park in two hours.

***

Looking back it's generally agreed that Blue Banshee Bridge was an unfortunate choice for Schatzi's plot-changing pow-wow. The name itself, *Blue Banshee Bridge*, referring to an Irish witch who brings death, should have been…".

Arf.

At first all went well. The five dogs under Schatzi's leadership agreed to recruit Jesus spotters among their immediate circle of canines, who would enlist their own coterie of canines, who would contact … and so on and so on. Special attention was to be given to dogs traveling abroad to spread the good woof. Unfortunately, one of the mutts, Arya (meaning evil dog), an Irish Blue Terrier, carried Schatzi's plan back to others of his kind precipitating the Great Dog Eat Dog War which…

"Which what Charly"?

"Which is too gruesome to …"

"But which creates reader interest in …"

"One dog chewing on another dog's leg? Rib? Tail? Snout"?

"Not just one dog. Hundreds of dogs. Thousands"?

Pause.

"Umm".

Cough.

Sneeze.

"So maybe…".

"We let that one go and move on"?

***

Meanwhile the CFD, Committee of Five Dogs, were working things out for themselves. Schatzi started by woofing "Arf, arf, …. Woof….. Arf…. Bowwowwow"? Namely; what did Jesus have in common with dogs? When one of the mutts woofed "Smell" the dogs agreed to alert their dog buddies to sniff around for the distinctive aroma of first century middle eastern perfumes which was used to wash Jesus's feet. Fortunately spikeNard, or simply Nard, which has a strong sweet house-filling aroma, is still around today. The problem for the committee is that Nard is extremely expensive. In today's market the perfume used to wash Jesus's feet would have cost $12,000. Whoa! Who in dog world had $12,000?

Pause.

More pause.

Woof… Gun…ther…

Who?

Gunther IV, world's richest dog. 32 plus millions. Gunther, once owned by Madonna in flowery Florida, a tongue panting, rear wriggling, tail-wagging, German shepherd was delighted to put up the money and CFD…

CHAPTER 15

THE WAR THAT WAS AND THE WAR THAT WASN'T

When Hannah and her two Stout Lads woke next morning they found themselves seated outdoors at the Tingle-Kringle café beside a diversely perceived figure.

Hannah smiled. Ahh. Nice to see Tarry O'Connor's lingering loveliness; reminding Hannah of her first love by the bonny banks of the river Nith. To Wigs he was an old pal from his summer days in the forest service, and to Hans the three headed hound, mentioned above.

"Madam President may we start with you"?

Hannah, lowered her head, shook off an annoying fly, and remained silent.

***

"Ludwig Schossenmeir"?

"Heinrich! Heinrich Hepplehardenstein Von Gruber! What a surprise. I'm dumbfounded. After, what is it? Ten years"?

***

While things have come to a standstill in our riveting narrative on earth, things aren't going any better above where Charly and Sam, two of our cosmic commentors, are having their own problems. Namely Charly's mindless rage; inwardly screaming obscenities whenever Jesus is mentioned.

"I can't help it, Sam. I try but…"

Woof.

"Caroline what's going on"?

"Don't fight it Charly. It's not your war".

"I thought we were beyond the tensions and terrors that plague our friends below".

"Obviously we're not. The war goes on even in our realm".

"Between"?

"Radical evil and radiant goodness".

Pause.

Cough.

Long pause.

"Even in you? But you're the…"

"Especially in me Charly. As I said before, I'm the devil's first enemy".

***

Meanwhile Schatzi was barking, yapping, woofing, the news that the fate of the long-legged feeders with soft hands and bad breath was now in the hands of dogworld. Find Jesus! But where to start? Dogs were of course all over. Too many to contact. What Schatzi needed was a canine committee to organize the search. Which brought her to the annual *Westminster Kennel Club Dog Show* in Madison Square Garden where, when she appeared in the front row with her American owner Arnold Really O'Reilly, she *caught the eye* (yuck!) of a sennenhund (a Bernese Swiss farm dog) currently in second place in the hound group, who barked back he'd slip his leash after BIS (Best in Show) was over and meet Schatzi in Central Park. Tossed out of the Garden for barking, Schatzi (and Arnold) took the tube downtown to the bowery where the *Marvelous Mutts* (the *Mixed Breeds Dog Shows of America*, for rescue dogs) were holding *their* annual event. After enlisting a dachshund-shih tzu, and several Heinz 57 mutts whose unrecorded ancestry remains - well unrecorded, it was agreed to meet uptown by the little-known Blue Banshee Bridge in Central Park in two hours.

***

Looking back it's generally agreed that Blue Banshee Bridge was an unfortunate choice for Schatzi's plot-changing pow-wow. The name itself, *Blue Banshee Bridge*, referring to an Irish witch who brings death, should have been…".

Arf.

At first all went well. The five dogs under Schatzi's leadership agreed to recruit Jesus spotters among their immediate circle of canines, who would enlist their own coterie of canines, who would contact … and so on and so on. Special attention was to be given to dogs traveling abroad to spread the good woof, and the inevitable traitors who would be hounded into silence.

"One dog chewing on another dog's leg? Rib? Tail? Snout"?

"Not just one dog. Hundreds of dogs. Thousands"?

Pause.

"Umm".

Cough.

Sneeze.

"So maybe…".

"We let that one go and move on"?

CHAPTER 16

THE HAIRY THREE-HEADED HOUND, WAITING TO WRITE, AND SPREADING THE GOOD WOOF

When Hannah and her two Bernese Stout Lads woke up the next morning they found themselves seated outdoors at the Tingle-Kringle café beside a diversely perceived figure.

To Hannah the bearded man with kind eyes reminded her of warm sunlight on her face and arms as she lay with her bonny young man on the banks of the river Nith. To Wigs he was an old pal from his summer days in the forest service, and to Hans the figure was Cerberus, the three headed dog who guards the gate to the land of the dead.

***

"Ludwig Schossenmeir"?

"Heinrich! Heinrich Hepplehardenstein Von Gruber! What a surprise. I'm dumbfounded. After, what is it? Ten years"?

***

Meanwhile Hans facing the three hairy-headed Cerberus, the horrifying hell hound from the underworld who guards the dear departed from escaping back into our world, steps back. He'd always liked dogs: loyal, protective…

Schatzi growled. "Grrrr. Snarl. Gr…" but froze when Cerberus, lunged forward eyes blazing, roared back **"Urah…yah hess ssss schlata. lata. Raa. Snapt snizzin Gar Gar Gar Dy Dy Dy!!!**

Seeing Cereberus had stopped short Hans held out his hands palms up, as he looked down, unable to hold his gaze on the three snarling heads and waited for Schatzi's translation.

"Ruff. … Ruff… Arf".

"Cerberus says he's a guard dog not an attack dog. He says we're to go back to our own people. Woof".

"Ask him why he has three heads".

Pause while the two, or is it four, dogs talked together.

"Ruff… woof, **arrrrah,** yip, **arrah, yip**. Pip…. Nez….Nargar…. **hellut** …. Nezzz. Holop".

"The first head says Stay Back; the second growls Ork-like incantations, and the third head's eyes spits sparks into anyone foolish enough to return his gaze".

***

Charly and Sam looking down on our riveting narrative are bewildered. What has Hannah's love life and a mythical three headed canine got to do with the search for Jesus?

"Charly"?

"I'm not sure what's going on. I know what's happening. We're in a haunted house with a thousand rooms that so far have nothing to do with the search for Jesus. There's the obligatory sex scene; a three-headed wild-eyed mythical canine; and Wiggy meets an old friend. Caroline"?

"Go back to Hannah's crew imprisoned in Bells Z's dark dungeon".

***

While things have come to a standstill in our riveting narrative on earth, things weren't aren't going any better above where Charly and Sam, two of our cosmic commentators, are having their own problems. Namely Charly's mindless rage inwardly screaming obscenities whenever the search for Jesus is alluded to.

"I can't help it, Sam. I try but…"

Woof.

"Caroline what's going on"?

"Don't fight it Charly. It's not your war".

"I thought we were beyond the tensions and terrors that plague our friends below".

"Obviously we're not. The war goes on even in our realm".

"Between"?

"Radical evil and radiant goodness".

Pause.

Cough.

Long pause.

"Even in you? But you're the…"

"Especially in me Charly. I'm the devil first enemy".

***

What's needed here is a comment on the commentators' conundrum. Is the author implying that Caroline is still struggling to do the right thing?

Woof.

Meanwhile Schatzi was woofing the news that the fate of the long-legged feeders with soft hands and bad breath was now in the hands of dogworld. Find Jesus! But where to start? Dogs were of course all over. Too many to contact. What Schatzi needed was a canine committee to organize the search. Which brought her to the annual *Westminster Kennel Club Dog Show* in Madison Square Garden where, when she appeared in the front row with her American owner Arnold Really O'Reilly, she *caught the eye* (yuck!) of a sennenhund (a Bernese Swiss farm dog) currently in second place in the hound group, who barked back he'd slip his leash after BIS (Best in Show) was over and meet Schatzi in Central Park. Tossed out of the Garden for barking Schatzi (and Arnold) took the tube downtown to the bowery where *Marvelous Mutts* (the *Mixed Breeds Dog Shows of America*), were holding *their* annual event. After enlisting a dachshund-shih tzu, and several Heinz 57 mutts whose unrecorded ancestry remains - well unrecorded, it was agreed to meet uptown by the little-known Blue Banshee Bridge in Central Park in two hours.

***

Looking back it's generally agreed that Blue Banshee Bridge was an unfortunate choice for Schatzi's plot-changing pow-wow. The name itself, *Blue Banshee Bridge*, referring to an Irish witch who brings death, should have been…".

Arf.

At first all went well. The five dogs under Schatzi's leadership agreed to recruit Jesus spotters among their immediate circle of canines, who would enlist their own coterie of canines, who would contact … and so on and so on. Special attention was to be given to dogs traveling abroad to spread the good woof

***

"Charly"?

Nods.

"How long is this going to drag on"?

"No! No dragons. No genetically altered atomic sea monsters oozing out of an oozy ocean lumbering through downtown Tokyo or New York idly eliminating…"

"Dragons aren't sea monsters. Godzilla's a sea monster".

Pause.

"Charly"?

"Umm".

"You do realize I'm due for a promotion. After thirty years".

"Sam. You're doing a great job. I have no complaints. How about Editor-in-Chief? Editor-in-Charge? Lord High Editor-in-Charge"?

"Stop it Charly. You're the real editor. I make suggestions and you toss most of them out".

"I can't believe this Sam".

"Of course you can. I'm only the early-options editor. I open the mail and toss the junk. You're editor-in-charge".

"Caroline"?

"He's got a point, Charly. You think you're it. You're just part of the process".

Pause.

"The conscious part. You're a conduit, a go-between, the middleman".

"Humm…"

"How did you start writing today"?

"I got up, dressed, ate, rested half my weight on my knees in my save-your-back slanted Zen chair and just started to write".

"Think again".

Pause.

"I read over what I'd written yesterday; then I started".

"Keep thinking".

Mini-pause.

"I waited for a few minutes. Then I began".

"Why wait? Why not just start"?

Pause.

"I was waiting till it felt right".

"What did you need to feel right"?

"I needed inspiration".

"What's inspiration? Not your conscious mind or else you wouldn't have to wait on it. It'd be right there whenever needed".

"Hum. So the Muse is my Unconscious"?

"Not entirely or you wouldn't even know there was a Muse".

"Go on".

"It's a relationship. Your consciousness is constantly conversing with images and ideas that compose your semi-consciousness, the subconscious – old memories, fears and hopes - ready to surface as needed. And…".

"And what"?

"And below the subconscious memories, fears and hopes lies the Unconscious. Which includes the possibility that a loving Higher Power waits to provide the wisdom and courage we need to live the lives we were created to live".

"You're saying consciousness is only part of the process? Which suggests that the far end of the Unconscious opens onto another dimension of reality".

"You got it Sam. Once you acknowledge the Unconscious the religious option is always available".

"Why? Freud uncovered the Unconscious, and he didn't find God. Most psychotherapists today don't find a Higher Power lurking in the hearts of their troubled clients".

"That's because they don't go far enough. Once the presenting problem is resolved their clients are out the door to resume their on-going lives".

"That doesn't prove anything Charly. My dreams tell me lots of weird things that aren't so in sunlight. Dreams aren't knowledge; dreams are passing fancies."

"Religion isn't about dreams, or knowledge".

"What is religion about if it's not about knowledge? Knowledge about the lofty out of sight Higher Power. God and Jesus, or some other uncertified phenomen ?"

Silence. Sam fidgets: rubbing his hands together, stretching his neck, and shifting his shoulders. Teeth clenched.

"Then what the hell is religion about? 'I believe in the Father, the Son and the Holy Spirit'. The Virgin Mary for Catholics. Being wafted into Heaven for evangelicals, while non-believers are gnashing their teeth in fiery Hell. Religion is nothing but a bundle of conflicting beliefs no reasonable person could accept. We know of course a man born in Israel preached and healed and was crucified by the Romans, but the bit about a return to life for forty days, being God's son, and so on is pure conjecture. It's a myth".

"Which might just be true".

"For you. Not for tons of other folks".

"Sam".

"Yes"?

"You're right. Any credible religion isn't about knowledge. It's about needing God. It's about having faith in a Higher Power – a Sovereign Source - who cares about the groaning creation. Especially human beings".

Pause.

"In fact, Sam, knowledge kills religion. And sometimes other human beings. Scientists have conflicting opinions on what's real, but no one dies if they're wrong. But if I know my religious beliefs are true and yours are false, I may defend my belief with forceful energy. Including at times…".

Sam pauses, presses his lips together, eyes closed, and drifts into worrisome reflection.

Time passes.

"Charly"?

"Humm"?

"Tell me about faith".

"Faith is belief without physical evidence".

"So if…".

Woof.

"What"?

WOOF!... arf…. Bow-wow….wooof.

"Schatzi says what about finding Jesus".

***

Sifting the negative reports on Nard tainted oddballs who might be Jesus Shatzi was left with three possibilities. One, the whole thing was a lost cause, spilt milk, a wild goose chase, water down the well, much ado about nothing …

Arf.

Two, Jesus exists but doesn't know it's time for him to come back to redeem God's "groaning creation". And three, Jesus is out there somewhere, and for some reason is keeping quiet about it.

CHAPTER 17

Arf... Woof... grrrr... sniff... Owwwwwlll... sniffff... sniff....

Growling, whining, howling, moaning, barking, sniffing, on and on it went as the Five Dogs discussed ways to trace Nard back to Jesus. Worldwide alert? Too public. Arya, Bells Z's poisonous pet, would surely notice. Pass the woof quietly to a small coterie of committed canines? Mingle with dogs sniffing for Nard and quietly follow up random rumors of human holiness, seems the best option.

And so it was Lou, a scrawny mixed-breed roaming the back streets in Central Penn, "the War Zone", in Albuquerque, where poverty, drugs, and gang violence are rampant, came upon a homeless man sleeping beside an abandoned warehouse. Crouching beside the man Lou, sniffed, lowered her head and licked the man's foul smelling, prickly warm face.

***

"Just as you did it to one of the least of these, who are my sisters and brothers, you did it to me."
Mt. 25:40.

Printed in the United States
by Baker & Taylor Publisher Services